Other books by Tish Thawer available

at Amazon.com, Barnes & Noble, and other online vendors

I0653073

<u>The Rose Trilogy</u>

Scent of a White Rose - Book 1

Roses & Thorns - Book 1.5

Blood of a Red Rose - Book 2

THE OVALELL SERIES

Aradia Awakens - Book 1

Prophecy's Child - Companion

The Rise of Rae - Companion

Shay and the Box of Nye - Companion

Praise for *Scent of a White Rose*

"Thawer managed what I thought was an impossible feat. She was able to put yet another new spin on the age old vampire tale." ~ The Bookshelf Sophisticate

"...everything about *Scent of a White Rose* was such a fresh new concept when it came to vampires, actually it was just a whole new concept in general for the paranormal genre! This is a read any paranormal lover should read!" ~ YA-Aholic

"*Scent of a White Rose* is not the plain Jane girl meets vampire and falls in love story...I will tell you that you should add this book to your TBR list." ~ The Book Nympho

"Tish Thawer crafts a seductive vampire tale with her eloquent writing style and keen sense of romance that simply entrances." ~ Romancing the Darkside

Praise for *Aradia Awakens*

"Tish Thawer is one of those authors whose works are marked by something incredibly special. With each book she writes, I am awed by the magickal elements in each novel." ~Author Rae Hachton

"The author skillfully weaves a tale so intense that you can't help but want more." ~The Cover and Everything in Between

"Once more, I was overwhelmed by the creativity and imagination that comes from this author..." ~Proserpine Craving Books

"I really, really like the world of Ovialell. The world is unique, complex, and full of all sorts of paranormal species. There are werewolves, vampires, amazons, Goddesses, there are so many interesting elements to the world." ~The Book Savvy Babe

Praise for *Aradia Awakens*

"Tish Thawer is one of those authors whose works are marked by something incredibly special. With each book she writes, I am awed by the magickal elements in each novel." ~Author Rae Hachton

"The author skillfully weaves a tale so intense that you can't help but want more." ~The Cover and Everything in Between

"Once more, I was overwhelmed by the creativity and imagination that comes from this author..." ~Proserpine Craving Books

"I really, really like the world of Ovialell. The world is unique, complex, and full of all sorts of paranormal species. There are werewolves, vampires, amazons, Goddesses, there are so many interesting elements to the world." ~The Book Savvy Babe

ACKNOWLEDGEMENTS

To my wonderful family: I love you. Thank you for supporting me throughout this journey. I can only hope that your continued faith and belief in me will remain as we begin the next one.

To Cortney: A simple thank you will have to do, because I don't have enough room to write everything that I'm grateful for when it comes to you!

To Regina Wamba: Thank you for all of your hard work. The beautiful images you've created have truly contributed to The Rose Trilogy's success.

To my editor Nancy Glasgow: Thank you for your keen eye and honest opinions. It's been a pleasure working with you.

Death of a Black Rose

Book three of The Rose Trilogy

PROLOGUE

(Rose)

After leaving Christian behind in Evie's office, I started to help set up the tables and chairs in the club. Suddenly, I felt my phone vibrating and looked down to see my dad's number.

The relief I felt was so overwhelming that I snapped the phone open, buzzing with excitement. "Dad. You're all right?"

"Yes, Rose. I'm fine."

"Oh, thank god. I was so worried that crazy bitch would hurt you when you told her you were leaving. Are you on your way to The Rising Pit now?"

A knot formed in my stomach when the line remained silent for just a little too long. "Rose, I need you to listen to me, baby. I know this will be hard to understand, but...I'm staying with Meredith. We're having a baby."

No words could flow past the anger now rising within me. I knew without a doubt Meredith had somehow tricked my dad into staying with her. *That bitch is going to pay.*

I launched the phone across the room and into a wall. It smashed into a million pieces. I threw chairs and crushed tables, seeing nothing but red from behind my glowing eyes. I couldn't control my demon side any longer. I didn't care if everyone knew, because the second I left here, I was going to kill Meredith and would probably never return.

Suddenly from behind me I heard Christian's voice. "Rose, my god, what's wrong?"

I spun around and stared at him through a crimson haze, trying to catch my breath. Even though I was angry, the sight of him had me wishing I had time to explain and apologize for everything. But I didn't.

Everyone was staring at me. I prepared to run for the door but Christian flew at me with his vampire speed and gripped me tightly. Before I could move he sank his fangs into my neck as I heard Evie scream, "Christian, NO!!!"

I had no control over my body going limp as the man I loved drank the life from me. Suddenly Christian's voice layered my mind. *"Your life to me, my life to you, through this bond our love is true. Whatever shall come, we share in whole. Life to death, eternity our*

goal."

As I took my last breath, something snapped inside my mind as we fell to the floor. The last thing I heard was Christian's voice inside my head. *"Rose, I forgive you."*

Rose's eyes open and then she's gone.

My life will be over before too long.

* * * * *

CHAPTER ONE

Scared

(Christian)

The moment the sun set, I awoke—alone. Rose was nowhere in sight.

"Rose, are you here?"

When I received no response I crawled out of bed and made my way into the bathroom. I looked from side to side, hoping to find some clue as to where she could be. The last thing I remembered was falling to the floor with her in my arms while our consort bond sealed her scanning ability into place. I felt the connection when it happened and sent my thoughts directly into her mind. I'd told her I forgave her, and I did. So the question remained...where was she now?

"She's gone, Christian."

I looked up into the mirror to see Loraine—Rose's mother—hovering behind me.

"I know. I can feel it. It's like our bond is being stretched." I sank down onto the bench where Rose always sat to do her makeup. I could still smell her scent in the air and my heart began to ache.

Loraine, who'd been killed by Meredith—the very demon that was currently bedding Rose's father—had recently started to appear in her ghostly form whenever she was needed or thought about. However, so far, I was the only one she could actually communicate with.

"Tell me what happened, Loraine."

"Well, after the two of you passed out upstairs, Evie had Dax and the others carry you both down to your room. They said it was too late to stop the process and that Rose would have to feed from you to complete the transition once you woke. You both remained unconscious for the rest of the night and all day today, but hours before sunset...Rose started to stir."

My head snapped up. "That's impossible. If she was finishing her transition she shouldn't have been able to wake until the sun went down. We should have woken at the same time."

"I know, Christian. I followed everyone down here last night and stayed with the two of you the whole time. Initially I was shocked when I saw her start to wake, but what I came to understand is that her demon side allows her to rise before the sun sets. Demons aren't confined to the night like vampires, and therefore neither is Rose. Once she'd risen, it was like she knew exactly what to do to complete the process." Loraine shook her head, ever so slightly. "I watched as she drank from you."

My hand flew to my neck and I could feel two small puncture wounds. Apparently Rose hadn't figured out how to use her sedative to heal me. That was something every Sire was supposed to teach their new sons or daughters, or in our case...wife. "She completed the process? She's a full vampire now?"

"I think so, but what I saw next scared me so much I must have disappeared. I only just came back when I felt you thinking of Rose."

I jumped up from the bench, my fists clenching and unclenching as my panic rose. Glancing back at the mirror I caught sight of myself; my hair and eyes had drifted dark. "Tell me everything, Loraine. What did you see that scared you?"

Bright silver streaks flowed down Loraine's cheeks and I realized she was crying. "She's bad, Christian. After she drank from you, I watched as my daughter's beautiful blonde hair turned dark as night, and her eyes became the deepest crimson I've ever seen. She's the hybrid now, and I'm scared for us all."

CHAPTER TWO

Lost

(Christian)

The decision to turn my girlfriend into a vampire was something I'd been planning to do for over a year. But what I hadn't planned on was turning her the moment I found out she was a demon. Talk about a shock. It had been a huge surprise and yet another secret she'd kept from me. But in that moment, I didn't have time to be mad; the instant I'd seen Rose's eyes glow red, I'd been flooded with the information about her heritage and the unwavering knowledge that turning her into the hybrid was the right thing to do—the only thing I *could* do. But now, as I stood frozen in place, looking into the depths of my inky black eyes, I hoped I hadn't made the wrong decision.

"Loraine, what happened next?"

"She rushed around in a frenzy, throwing stuff into a bag, and then flew out of the club. I haven't felt a pull toward her since." Loraine sobbed, causing my heart to break even more.

I paced back into the bedroom, feeling completely lost—
lost without Rose, lost in what I should do...just completely and
utterly lost. Suddenly a knock on the door stopped my
depressive spiral.

"Christian, may we come in?" called Evie.

I wasn't in the mood to face everyone right now, but knew
I didn't have a choice. "Yes, come in."

The door slowly opened and Evie and Dax hesitantly
entered. I was relieved it was just the two of them. They eyed
me cautiously as I sat down on the bed and buried my head in
my hands.

"Are you...all right?" Evie's voice was tentative.

She was probably scared that I'd permanently drifted dark
and was in the throes of Rose's poisonous blood. "Don't worry,
I'm fine." I tried to assure her.

"But your hair, your eyes..."

I flew from the bed, startling everyone, and started to pace
again. "I've drifted dark because I'm upset! Rose is gone."

Evie's gasp signaled that she hadn't registered the fact that we were alone in the room. Dax frowned and sank down onto the bed, claiming the spot I'd just vacated.

"What do you mean gone? What's happened? There's so much I don't understand."

I wasn't sure if I should tell them about Loraine, but in order for my explanation to make sense I really didn't have any other choice. "I know, Evie. There's a lot of information I have that you don't. Why don't we go upstairs to your office and I'll explain." I had to get out of this room, because staying in it— without Rose here—was starting to trigger some dark emotions that I couldn't risk facing right now.

As we made our way out of my room and down the stark, white-tiled hall, I sent my thoughts to Loraine. *"I have to tell her everything. About Rose and Jeremy being demons, about you, about my decision to turn Rose into the hybrid...everything."*

"I know, Christian. I just hope that they will understand and not be scared into a reaction that would hurt Rose or Jeremy...or you." The look on her face was grim as she gently floated beside me.

Once we reached the private entrance that led into Evie's office, we all climbed the stairs, our silence filling the small space. As the bookcase closed behind us, Evie and Dax took a seat on the couch that sat against the far wall, while I continued to pace. Loraine hovered by the door and nodded to me encouragingly. I wasn't sure where to start, so I tried to organize my thoughts into a timeline that would be easy to follow.

"As you're both aware, I developed extra *abilities* during my triggering which allow me to hear and know things that others don't. The latter actually floods my mind with information about situations with unwavering clarity and finality. This was how I knew what to do when Evie was knocked unconscious."

They both nodded their heads and I continued.

"Recently, my abilities, in combination with something else, have helped me to understand a lot about everything that's been happening."

Evie shifted in her seat as Dax put his arm around her shoulders. I was sure they knew what was coming next was going to be hard to swallow.

"For a few weeks now, Rose's mother, Loraine, has been able to visit and communicate with me from the other side."

Dax visibly sank further into the couch as he exhaled a shocked breath, and Evie's hair started to drift at a rapid pace. This was not going well.

"Don't panic. She's been a huge help. Please just listen and let me explain."

CHAPTER THREE

Fate

(Christian)

"When Loraine was alive, she possessed an ability that allowed her to calm people by her mere presence. It's because of this power that I think she and I can connect. Basically, I'm able to see and hear her because we both share some sort of psychic ability.

"She explained that each time she materializes, her mind—much like mine, is flooded with information about current situations. It's like the gods give her a data dump every time she returns to this plane. This is how she found out that Rose and Jeremy are demons."

Evie and Dax visibly tensed up but thankfully remained silent and allowed me to continue without interruption.

"Rose had no idea about her heritage until the night she fought with Meredith. Ever since then she's carried this secret and for the last few months, tried to distance herself from me in an effort to keep us all safe. It wasn't until Jeremy told her he was staying with Meredith because she's pregnant, that Rose lost control of her demon side. That's what you witnessed when she flew into her fit of rage.

"Now, I know you don't agree and have no way to understand my choice, but in that instant, I knew turning her and making her my consort was the only thing that would save us all. She's now the hybrid we need to defeat Meredith."

I took a deep breath and stared at Evie and Dax. My rapid revelations eased about a hundred pounds off my shoulders, but the unsure looks plastered on both their faces, combined with their increased drifting, left me unsure as to where things stood.

After a deep breath of her own, Evie spoke. "Christian, while I'm well aware of and do understand your extra abilities, I'm sitting here looking at your dark hair and eyes and wondering exactly how turning Rose was the best thing for our clan? If her blood causes you to drift *permanently* dark, that means we will have lost our new Sire, and personally, I can't think of anything worse."

I knew she wasn't trying to reprimand me for my decision, but instead, simply sharing her concerns. And they were valid concerns, but again, the knowledge I possessed still led me to believe that turning Rose was the right thing to do.

"I can't explain how I know it, but I'm telling you, turning Rose will save our clan. Balam said we needed to create a hybrid to fight the demons, and then all of a sudden it turns out that the woman I love *is* a demon...somehow I don't think that's a coincidence. Call it cosmic intervention or fate, whatever, but I know I made the right choice."

Evie stood up and came to stand directly in front of me.

"Well, *fate* is a pretty big leap, and one that you've left us no choice but to take. But Christian, you're a vampire and the consort bond also means that you can't be away from your chosen for very long. What happens if she doesn't come back? You do realize that you'll die because of your connection now, don't you?"

I turned away, catching a glimpse of Loraine before I answered Evie's question. Rose's mom looked as nervous as I felt.

"Yes, I'm very aware of our connection, and while it's being stretched, it's not severed, which means she's still alive. As long as I find her soon, we should both be just fine."

Evie looked at Dax and I watched him shake his head while she lifted an eyebrow. I knew they were scanning each other's thoughts and having a private conversation; probably about how they agreed that I'd completely lost my mind.

"Look, I'm going to start my search for Rose immediately with Loraine's help, so if you can get Renard to cover my duties tonight, I'd appreciate it."

"Speaking of the clan, I think it's important that you speak to them before you leave. Obviously the cat's been let out of the bag that you're the new Sire and they deserve an explanation," Evie stated.

"Yes, of course. You're right." As I turned to head toward the door, I remembered something else I needed to share. "By the way, Terrance already knows I'm the new Sire. He was still in the pit when I delivered the true death to Kennedy."

Evie dropped her head, obviously frustrated that I'd ruined our element of surprise.

"I'm sorry, Evie. I know this changes everything, but I promise it will all work out."

"I hope so, Christian. I truly hope so."

A knock on the door interrupted our conversation. "Come in," Evie called.

Dominique entered the room with a worried look on her face. "Um...we've all fed from the blood bags downstairs and just wanted to check and make sure everything was all right since we didn't see any of you in the pit."

Evie had confined all of us to feeding from blood bags after a vampire named Kennedy bit a demon in the club last week, causing him to drift dark. Unbeknownst to us at the time, that demon had been Rose, which was another tidbit of information I gleaned as our bond took hold. From that point on, we'd all been feeding from blood bags as not to risk any of us falling prey to another accident, but more specifically, in case Meredith started sending demons to purposely infect us by posing as willing donors.

Evie cast a quick look in my direction. "Yes, we're fine. Please let everyone know we'll be out in a few moments."

CHAPTER FOUR

Good Enough

(Christian)

I followed Evie and Dax out of the office and found myself under the sudden scrutiny of the people I'd considered my family for centuries.

Bobby, my best friend, was sitting on the bottom step of the staircase that led to the second story of the club, while Renard and his wife, Loni, sat at one of the tables in the middle of the room. Dominique and her sister, Tori, were standing behind the bar as usual, and Terrance was leaning against the wall beside the entrance.

I walked across the room and up the steps toward the front door, putting myself slightly higher than the small crowd in an effort to make my first talk as Sire seem more "official." As I moved close to Terrance, he kindly slapped me on the shoulder before I turned around to face everyone.

"Um...I guess you all realize that I'm your new Sire." I cringed at their silent nods and *humphs* but continued. "Evie chose to perform the Passing of Powers ritual in an effort to prepare for our upcoming battle with the demons. We thought that having two Sires to fight against them instead of one was the best plan. I'm sorry we didn't tell you, but the idea was to keep it a secret so we'd gain the upper hand. Obviously I kind of blew that."

The blank stares I received had me swallowing hard against the lump in my throat.

"As you all witnessed, Rose is a demon, and while I'm sure you won't understand my reasoning, I know that by turning her into our hybrid and my consort, we will be able to defeat Meredith and her growing army."

The silence that hung in the air was finally broken when Dominique spoke up. "So even though you're showing signs of drifting dark, we're all just supposed to believe that turning Rose will somehow save us?"

"I'm hoping that you can trust me enough as your new Sire to do just that, yes. The abilities that I've developed have given me clear insight into the fact that Rose will be our saving grace."

"Then where the fuck is she?" Bobby demanded. "Besides, like Dom said, you're standing there with dark hair and eyes. What's gonna stop you from foaming at the mouth now that Rose's demon blood is running through your veins?"

"I won't pretend that I didn't start to feel the effects of her blood as I drank her to the brink of death. But the instant our connection snapped into place, everything changed. I knew I'd be able to survive this, and so will she."

It was then that Terrance spoke up. "Listen, if Rose's blood was truly affecting him like Meredith's did me, he wouldn't even be able to think or talk about her right now, so why don't you all cut him some fucking slack. He's our new Sire, and if he says that things will be okay, then that should be good enough."

His statement caught everyone off guard. And while I was definitely grateful that he'd come to my defense, it was still a pretty big shock. I wondered if the fact that Loraine was hovering near him was part of the reason he seemed so "pro-me."

After a few seconds of watching everyone contemplate his words, Dominique spoke up again. "I'm not trying to be a bitch here, but I have to ask, you said that you're *our* new Sire? I thought once a new Sire assumes power, they leave with their consort to start a clan of their own."

Thankfully, Evie responded to Dominique's statement. "Yes, Dom, that is usually the case, but since we are on the brink of something that none of us understand, I thought it would be best if Christian and Rose remain with our clan until things have been resolved with the demons. Especially since Rose is now our best chance of winning against them."

"Fine. So back to Bobby's question. Where in the hell is she?" Dominique repeated.

The tension in the air was thick and telling them Rose was now the hybrid had sucked. However, admitting that I had no idea where she was, or what state of mind she was currently in, was going to be the hardest part of all.

"I'm not sure. Since Rose is able to rise before sunset, my guess is that she left to go check on her father."

The room erupted as everyone flew from their seats and started shouting.

"WHAT? That's suicide! She may be the hybrid now, but walking straight into Meredith's grasp has to be the dumbest idea ever," Bobby declared.

"What the fuck, Evie, how could you let this happen?" Tori demanded.

Renard and Loni were huddled together, probably plotting their exit strategy, while Dominique simply glared in my direction.

"STOP!" This was only the second time I'd used my Sire command, and while I definitely agreed with all of their concerns, I had to maintain a confident exterior. "All of your concerns are completely valid, which is why I'm going to have to cut this short. I'm headed straight there to make sure Rose doesn't run into Meredith right off the bat." I didn't really know if this was where Rose had gone, but I sure as hell wasn't going to tell them that.

As I turned away, Terrance piped up and asked the one question I wanted to avoid at all costs. "Do you want me to go with you?"

Thankfully, once again, Evie came to my rescue. "Actually, I think it's going to be important that Christian goes alone. For one, the less people for Meredith to take notice of, the better, but also because Rose and Christian haven't been able to come together as consorts yet, since she left before he woke tonight."

Terrance nodded and luckily everyone else started to disperse to begin their nightly duties to open the club. Evie winked at me before engaging Dominique in a new conversation, providing me the time I needed to slip out the front door.

I didn't have to think about Loraine, because she was already hovering right beside me. *"Do you really think Rose went straight to Jeremy's?"* she asked.

"I'm not sure, Loraine. But right now, it's the best idea I've got."

CHAPTER FIVE

Bad

(Rose)

Waking up next to Christian was nothing new. But waking up next to Christian with my teeth throbbing, and an uncontrollable urge to sink them into his neck, was definitely a shock.

I literally couldn't help myself as I bent his head to the side and sunk my newly developed fangs through the soft flesh of his throat. The sensation of his warm blood filling my mouth was absolute heaven. I could also feel our consort bond and instantly realized that was the reason I couldn't resist the temptation to drink. This was how all *newbies* completed their transition and drifted to their "normal" coloring.

I raised my head from the side of Christian's neck and knew something was wrong. Wrong, because I wasn't just a vampire...I was also a demon.

Flying from the bed, I looked into the mirror. My hair had drifted completely black and my eyes were a deep crimson. In the vampire world this meant I was "bad." But thinking about Meredith, and the fact that she'd killed my mom and was now basically holding my dad prisoner...bad was suddenly feeling pretty damn good.

Racing around the room, I gathered some supplies and threw them into a bag. I looked over at Christian, surprised he was still comatose but then noticed the clock on the nightstand—it read 3:24 p.m., still hours before sunset. I assumed it was my demon side that allowed me to wake; the demon side that I'd hid from everyone until my father fell prey to that bitch. The moment that he'd called and told me that he was staying with her because they were having a *baby*, I'd snapped.

With that memory now fueling my anger, I ran out of the club not caring if I was bad or not. I couldn't wait to get to my dad's and kill Meredith, and thanks to Christian, I was now the one person who could make it happen. I raced between the trees that lined the freeway to Masen. The feeling of the wind blowing through my now black hair was so freeing that I almost flew past my exit. I knew my dad lived off of 29th Street, thanks to Renard and Loni's recent reconnaissance mission.

I raced into the open space across from their brownstone, but realized it was early evening and both my dad and the bitch would most likely still be at work. As I contemplated my next move, the rumble in my stomach brought the fact that I was completely famished into sharp relief. The little blood I'd taken from Christian was just enough to complete my transition, but definitely not enough to appease my growing appetite.

After all those months of talking to Terrance, even though he'd been under Meredith's influence at the time, I did learn a lot about vampires. For one, they didn't feed from others of their kind, only humans, and only once per night. They programmed the sedative that flowed from their fangs to erase the person's mind and to heal their wounds. This made the experience something that was only a necessity for the vampires and never left the human hurt, or even aware that it had happened at all. Too bad I'd run out before Christian had a chance to teach me how to do any of that. I figured it should be pretty easy and since I didn't have a choice but to feed, now was as good a time as any to learn.

I looked around the park and saw a few people milling about. There was a young couple pushing a baby stroller on the far side of the small lake; an old woman sitting on the bench of the nearest shore, feeding the birds; but it was the jogger that was headed down the path that ran straight under the stone bridge that caught my eye. The bridge ran through a small grove of maple trees which shaded the entire length. It was perfect.

I made sure no one was looking my way, then raced to the other end of the tunnel and waited in the shadows under the bridge. As the man got closer, I could smell his cologne mixed with his sweat, but it was the sweet smell of his blood that had my fangs aching again.

As soon as he was within reach, I grabbed him and pushed him back against the curved stone wall. I moved so fast, that he didn't have a chance to protest before my fangs were buried deep in his neck. I prepared to think the thoughts I assumed would program my sedative, but instead got completely lost in the taste of his blood. I stifled his screams with my hand and continued to suck deep draws of blood down my throat. It felt as if his blood was a drug, one that I would never be able to break the habit of. It was more than just a vampire necessity, it was like his blood was the life essence that was fueling my body and turning me into something that Meredith would fear. I loved it. I didn't stop drinking until the man fell to the ground.

CHAPTER SIX

Happily Ever After

(Meredith)

It had only been two days since I'd forged the mind bond with Jeremy by forcing him to drink my blood. He'd left me no choice when he prepared to walk out on me and our baby. Now, I only had to slip him a little of my blood every day to maintain control. And, since before this little hiccup, we really *were* in love, it didn't take much to nudge him into feeling as if we were living out our happily ever after.

"Jeremy, darling. What time do you think you'll be home from work tonight?" I asked as I cleaned off the kitchen table.

"I'm not sure, honey. My boss said since I missed our last meeting in Seela, he wanted to make up for it today with a conference call." He shook his head, as if still trying to piece together the events of that day.

I still didn't know *exactly* how Jeremy had found out about our heritage or from whom, even though the answer seemed pretty obvious. All I knew for sure was that he'd cancelled his trip to Seela, came home early that day, and found me killing Damien in our garage. It had been the worst way possible to expose him to our demon side. But thankfully, that was all behind us now.

"Okay, well, just give me call when you're close to heading home so I'll know when to put dinner on."

"Don't you have one of your meetings tonight?" he asked.

I tensed up at the question, my eyes flaring red as I set the dishes in the sink. I hadn't talked to or seen any of the other demons who'd been coming to my meetings since after I'd received a call from Damien's cousin, Raúl. He told me that Damien's body had been found down by the railroad tracks. I feigned surprise, of course, seeing as I was the one who dumped him there.

Damien had practically forced me to kill him when the power hungry fool threatened to murder Jeremy. Plus, I refused to have a lieutenant who thought he could overpower me or uproot my plans. I told Raúl to let me know when the funeral was so I could come pay my respects, but my real reason for wanting to go was so I could get some time alone with him. I was hoping that he'd agree to step into Damien's shoes as my second in command. I had to get back to building my army, because I knew Rose and her adopted vampire family would soon be closing in on me.

"No. This week's meeting has been postponed, so I'll be here waiting for you." I turned back toward Jeremy and rubbed a hand over my belly.

With a loving smile, he laid his hand on top of mine and kissed my cheek. "Sounds great. I'll call you when my day is over."

Watching him head out the door with his coffee mug in hand, left me with a satisfied feeling. He'd be sipping my blood all the way to work, and therefore, my mind bond would remain safely in place. The realization that I would never lose the man I loved was almost as euphoric as when I'd drained the life from his wife.

Jeremy was the first demon outside of my family that I'd ever run across. The moment we'd met, I knew I wanted him to be the father of my child. The idea of continuing my pure demon bloodline thrilled me, but the first step I'd had to take was to eliminate his wife. Her life essence had flowed into me and activated my ancient demon traits: faster speed, enhanced strength, and most importantly, my journey to becoming immortal. My grandmother's stories rang in my ears as I'd stood over Loraine's dead body; stories of our ancestors drinking human blood. It was in that instant that I knew I'd found the key to becoming the most powerful demon in existence.

Now, if I could just go to this funeral and get Raúl to fall in line, I could start up the meetings again and continue to spike the punch with human blood. Most of the other demons didn't have a clue as to what they were drinking, but they had certainly enjoyed the "uplifting" effects it had on them. Raúl and a few other cousins had been in on the plan, and after demonstrating their slight increase in strength and speed, I knew dosing them in small amounts was the best way to build my unsuspecting army. However, before I could do anything else, I had to make the doctor's appointment that would confirm my pregnancy. I'd been so happy when my home test appeared positive, but with the distraction of killing Damien and having to establish my mind bond with Jeremy, the last couple of days had been a complete blur.

As I headed up the stairs to retrieve my cell phone, I realized that even though Jeremy and I had just shared breakfast, I was still famished. The problem was...I wasn't hungry for food.

I was only drinking human blood as a way to maintain my demon traits, but right now I felt more like a vampire, like I was actually craving it. I entered our bedroom and picked up my cell off the nightstand, wondered if my appetite was something I should be worried about. It only took a moment for my uncertainty to grow, so instead of dialing the number for my doctor, I punched the numbers for my grandmother instead.

"Good morning, Grandma, it's Meredith. I was wondering if you'd be up for a visit today?"

"Of course, child. You should know you're always welcome here. No need to call first."

The sound of my grandmother's voice was like a soothing balm to my soul. She was the one person in our family who had special gifts that were inherent to our demon race. But to me, her most special gift was how loved and comfortable she had always made me feel. I just hoped that she'd remain as calm and comforting if I decided to tell her what was truly going on.

CHAPTER SEVEN

Disappointment

(Christian)

I continued to contemplate my little speech as I drove down the freeway in my '67 Comet Caliente. I had hoped it would ease the disappointment I knew my clan felt, but after scanning them as we spoke, the doubts and fears that layered their thoughts were pretty overwhelming. In their eyes, not only was turning Rose a terrible idea, but the fact that I was the new Sire and they hadn't known about it was most likely going to cause a problem for quite some time.

In an effort to distance myself from these thoughts, I looked over at the passenger seat and saw Loraine staring out the windshield. It was so odd to look at someone and yet still be able to see right through them. The trees were flying by the window as ethereal wisps of her hair blew in a wind that I wasn't even sure she could feel.

"Don't worry, Loraine. We'll find her."

She turned to face me and smiled a sad smile. "I know, Christian. I'm just concerned about how she will be *when* we find her."

I knew Loraine was talking about the fact that Rose had drifted dark when she'd completed her transition. Most people rose as light vampires, but there were instances where, if the person carried sorrow and pain within them from their human lives, they would show signs of that by drifting darker initially. With everything that Rose had been through over the last year––her mother's death, finding out about vampires, her attempted murder of Meredith, and the revelation that she and her dad were demons—um, yeah, I supposed I shouldn't be surprised that she turned out darker than expected. Now it was just a matter of reaching her in time, before her emotions shut down, because at that point she'd truly be lost to us.

The horrible images playing in my head had me veering onto the shoulder. I couldn't imagine my sweet Rose as some dark, evil creature. The idea caused a serious knot in my stomach because now, it was *my* responsibility to kill any vampire who drifted dark, even if it was the love of my life.

"Dammit," I cussed, banging my fist against the steering wheel. "Why couldn't I have been there to help her through her transition like every other Sire in history?"

Loraine's ghostly hand settled on top of my shoulder. "Christian, I'm sorry. I didn't mean to upset you with my worries. And you already know the answer to that. Rose is special. She's now the hybrid and that means there's bound to be differences with her transition than any other's before her."

"Yes, but now, I'm just so scared that what seemed like the right thing to do at the time was possibly the worst decision I could've made."

Loraine's weak smile didn't offer much comfort, but apparently her calming ability still worked wonders, because as soon as the words left my mouth, the doubts about my decision eased, if only slightly.

Getting back on topic, I asked, "Have you felt any kind of pull toward Rose or Jeremy recently?"

"No. I haven't." She shook her head and dropped her hand back into her lap.

I wanted to reassure her that everything would be okay, but I couldn't bring myself to lie to her. I honestly didn't know if we'd be able to find Rose or save Jeremy, but whatever our futures held, I had a feeling there was going to be a lot of heartache along the way.

* * * * *

(Rose)

After savoring the last drop of blood as it ran down my throat, I looked down at the man I'd just killed. I wasn't sure what to do or what I should be feeling. As a good vampire I should be mortified; as a bad vampire I should be reveling in the kill; and as a demon I should apparently feel the man's life force filling me with an immortal essence. But as the hybrid, I felt nothing. I wasn't remorseful, I wasn't sad, I wasn't happy, I wasn't...*anything*.

Black hair surrounded my face as I closed my eyes and tried to force myself back on task. I'd come here to end Meredith and save my dad, but I found myself no longer caring. I lifted my head and opened my eyes. Maybe I should destroy the bridge in an effort to conceal the dead man's body. Then again, why should I care if he was discovered or not? If anyone approached me for any reason, whether it was to ask the time or to accuse me of murder, I had nothing to fear. Nothing or no one could threaten me now.

Indifference layered my brain as I wiped my mouth, then rubbed away the traces of blood against my jeans. I walked out from underneath the bridge and everything looked different. It all seemed more crisp and clear...heightened somehow. I could hear squirrels scurrying throughout the trees, and the wheels of the stroller crunching over the rocks in its path. The old woman was still sitting in the same spot, feeding the birds, and even though I was at least one-hundred yards away, I could hear the low clucking noise she made under her breath as she scattered the seeds on the ground in front of her.

It was amazing. The sky was bluer than blue, and the trees

swayed in time with music that I was sure no one else could

hear. For being dead, I suddenly felt so alive. I wanted to race

around the park, up the trees, through the city, leap from

building to building, crush cars with my bare hands, or maybe

even stop a train. I laughed out loud at the thought, causing the

police officer who'd rounded the corner to turn in my

direction.

The low hiss that escaped my lips was a shock to both me

and him. However, I was long gone before the cop had a

chance to blink. I now watched from my perch in the top of

one of the tall trees as the idiot spun around, looking from side

to side. It didn't take him long to find the dead man's body and

within minutes the park was surrounded by flashing lights.

Yellow tape went up and all the people I'd noticed before were

being gathered and questioned. Each of them reported that

they hadn't seen anything or anyone unusual. A wicked smiled

crept across my face at the idea that any of them could have

been my dinner, and yet none of them had even seen me.

I continued to watch as a crowd started to gather and the man's body was wheeled out on a gurney from underneath the bridge. It was in a black coroner's bag, just like you'd see on TV. I tried to muster some sort of emotion, but as I watched the corpse being loaded into the black van, I still felt nothing. It wasn't until I saw my dad's Lexus pull into his driveway across the street did I feel a twinge of anything. Unfortunately for him, the only thing I felt now was disgust.

I stared at the house as Meredith came out the front door and greeted my dad on the lawn with a hug and kiss. They stood there for a while, watching the scene in the park unfold. Finally, my dad walked across the street and asked a police officer exactly what had happened. The officer hesitated at first, but once Dad explained that they lived directly across the street, he started to share bits of information. After giving a serious nod to the cop, Dad walked back across the street and embraced Meredith once more.

Finally a feeling sparked within me—one of rage. I had come here to kill Meredith and "save" my dad, but watching as the happy couple walked back into their perfect little home caused something inside me to snap. I could literally feel my emotions shutting down. As I watched them cross the threshold, I was suddenly over this entire thing—just like my dad had apparently gotten over me. As sad as that should make me, I couldn't bring myself to care anymore. I was a completely different person now and it was obvious that so was he.

I took one last look at my dad's house then disappeared into the night.

CHAPTER EIGHT

Stories

(Meredith)

Once I hung up with my grandmother, I showered and got dressed. I was still off from work due to the "illness" I'd faked a couple of days ago. I wanted to talk to her and make sure my baby was okay before I headed back to an office filled with nosy co-workers. Plus, I figured once I returned, announcing I was pregnant would make perfect sense as to why I had needed the time off.

On my way across town to Grandma's house I tried to think of the best way to get the information I needed without openly admitting I was drinking human blood. As much as she knew about the ancient stories, I highly doubted that learning her only granddaughter was openly practicing them would make for a very pleasant visit.

As I pulled my BMW into her drive, I saw her peek out from the kitchen window and give a little wave. I walked straight in, knowing she'd have already unlocked the door for me.

"Hi, Grams," I called out.

"Hello, honey. Come on in. I'm making your favorite."

Grandma's back was to me as she continued to wash dishes in the sink. I could smell the herbs from the roasted chicken and stuffed green peppers drifting from the oven, but instead of my mouth watering as usual, my stomach rolled. *Dammit.*

It was becoming more and more obvious that my decision to become immortal was starting to have negative affects in addition to the positive ones. Yes, I may be strong, fast, and immune to harm, but apparently I was also becoming something else in the process.

Not wanting to show my sudden concern, I took a seat at the kitchen table and said, "Smells good."

"I'm happy to see you, Meredith, it's been a while. How did you manage to make it over during the week?"

"Well, that's part of what I wanted to talk to you about. I

haven't been feeling well, and I think it's because I may be pregnant."

Grandma gasped, and spun to face me. "What?"

I smiled and placed a hand upon my stomach. "Yep. I think I may be pregnant with Jeremy's child."

"Jeremy is the man you've told me about? The demon who doesn't know he's a demon."

"Yes." I giggled.

Grandma took the seat next to me and reached for my hands. I waited as she held them tight and closed her eyes. I knew she was trying to use her gifts to sense the baby, but I was a little nervous at exactly what she'd pick up.

After a few moments of strained silence, Grandma released me. "Well, you're right. You are pregnant." She sat back in her chair and smiled, but I could tell something was off when it didn't quite reach her eyes. "I'm not sure of the sex and I can't quite get a good visual, but it's definitely a pure-blood demon. The question is...why do I sense human blood in your system?"

Well, shit. So much for keeping my secret. I wanted to open up to her but was worried about her reaction to my news, so I decided to skew the truth just a bit. "Grams, please understand. I didn't mean for it to happen. Recently I was severely injured, but after remembering all the stories you told me about our ancestors, I drank human blood in a desperate attempt to save my own life. It worked. I healed almost immediately and gained major amounts of strength and speed." I waited to see what she'd say before I continued to dig this hole.

With a sadness layering her features, she sat there frowning like grandmas do. "Well, I can't say that I'm pleased, or that I have any idea what this will do to you or your baby. But I can tell that you are changing, and I'm afraid that what you've started will not be good for our race." She pushed away from the table and returned to the sink. I felt like shit as she turned the oven off, obviously realizing I wouldn't be eating any of the food she'd cooked.

"I'm sorry." I didn't know what else to say, and I did feel bad for letting her down. But not only was stopping what I started out of the question, I literally didn't think that I could stop if I wanted to. Grandma was right, I had changed, and now there was no going back.

I tentatively approached my grandma as she methodically scrubbed the dishes in the sink, and gave her a small hug from behind. I wasn't sure if this would be the last time I would see her or not, but I left the house without another word. I hoped she would be able to accept my decisions once I proved that becoming immortal wasn't a bad thing, but a good one. Who knows, maybe she would start drinking human blood too, and then we could be together forever. The idea had merit but I wasn't holding out hope.

I let the thought drop as I backed out of the driveway, switching my focus to happier things. It was only two in the afternoon, so I decided to head to the store to pick up what I'd need for dinner. I couldn't wait to welcome Jeremy home in the special way I'd done over the last few days: a glass of wine for him laced with my blood, candles, and sexy lingerie.

Our lives had become so much better since I'd started controlling him. I'd wiped his memory of me killing Damien and about us being demons. As far as he knew, we were just a happy couple in love who were getting ready to have a baby. I did, however, decide to leave the memories of when I'd comforted him after Loraine's death. That way, he'd truly feel the depth of our connection. But, the one thing I didn't hesitate on doing while creating our perfect world, was to erase all his memories of Rose. I couldn't risk any memories of her leaking through, especially if she was the one who'd told him about me and all that I'd done.

Shaking off all thoughts of the past, I finished my grocery shopping then headed straight home and began marinating the steaks when my cell phone began to ring.

"Hello."

"Hi, Meredith. It's Raúl. I was calling to let you know that Damien's service will be tomorrow afternoon at The Angelus Funeral Home on East 16th at four p.m."

"Okay, thank you, Raúl. I'll see you there." I hung up the phone, smiling. I was well aware that tomorrow would be hard for everyone in Damien's family, and therefore I'd have to be sure to put on an especially good act. My plan was to get through the service, then speak to Raúl alone. From the way he'd handled digesting the human blood at the meeting, I thought he'd make a good replacement for his dead cousin.

As I continued to contemplate my plan, I headed back to the kitchen to start the vegetables for dinner, but just as I sat the pan on the stove I saw flashing lights outside the front window. I walked into the living room and saw the park across the street being surrounded by cops and other emergency vehicles. I stood watching as they taped off the area around the stone bridge, and then took a shocked breath when they wheeled out a dead body.

A few minutes later, Jeremy pulled into the driveway. I walked out the front door and greeted him with a hug and kiss. We stood there together, watching the police scurry around the scene. Finally when a cop walked out toward his squad car,

Jeremy crossed the street to speak with him. After a few minutes he walked back across the street, hugged me, then led me into the house.

"Apparently there was a man attacked under the bridge. The officer said his neck had been torn at and he died from major blood loss."

The instant I heard the words neck and blood, my eyes flared red. Thankfully, Jeremy was behind me as we walked back into the kitchen, and didn't notice.

I could only think of one thing that would tear out someone's neck and leave them to bleed to death. Well, besides myself—make that two things. I instantly worried this was a message from Christian's clan. I forced myself to remain calm and continued to prepare our dinner. I couldn't let Jeremy see that I was actually on the verge of losing control.

"Did they say if there were any suspects?" I asked.

"No. The officer said that no one in the park noticed anyone strange or heard anything. I guess we'll just have to watch the news and see if they found something to go on once they've completed the investigation."

"Well, I don't know about you, but the idea of people being killed in the park across the street from where we'll be raising our baby isn't the most comforting thing. Maybe we should think about moving."

Jeremy spun around, his eyes wide. "Really? You've lived here for so long. You'd really consider uprooting after just one crime in the park?"

"Well, yes! I may have lived here for a long time, but I've never been pregnant before, and certainly never had to worry about anyone else's safety but my own. But now...I couldn't imagine our child walking home from school and seeing something like this, or worse, being the victim."

Running was never really my style, but with the meetings on hold and the vampires obviously closing in, moving somewhere else might not be a bad idea right now. "What do you think? Maybe we could move into one of the high rises downtown that has around the clock security."

Jeremy walked over and pulled me into an embrace.

"Honey, I'll move wherever you want as long as you feel safe.

Plus, if we moved downtown, we'd both be closer to work, so

it would offset the increased cost of housing if we didn't have

to drive to work every day."

I was glad he was seeing things my way. "Thank you,

sweetheart. I'll call the realtor tomorrow."

CHAPTER NINE

Warn Me

(Christian)

We arrived at the address that Renard and Loni had provided in their report and I parked the car directly across the street from Jeremy and Meredith's brownstone. The block was quiet, except for a few people that I now realized were cops walking through the park. They seemed to be gathering yellow tape from around the bridge. Police, crime tape...this was not looking good. I had a sinking feeling that whatever happened had something to do with Rose.

"Loraine, are you able to check to see if Jeremy and Meredith are in their home?"

"No, Christian. I'm sorry. I can only go where other people's thoughts pull me, and like I said, I haven't felt anything from Jeremy for a while."

"All right then, I'm going to wait until the police clear the vicinity, then go check out what's happening in the park. After that we'll head over to the brownstone."

I figured I'd need to check out the park first in case that's where Rose had confronted Meredith. But for now, I had no choice but to wait in the car. I thought about making small talk with Loraine, but I just didn't know what to say. I had so many questions about Rose and their family but I didn't want to appear insensitive by making her talk about the loved ones she'd lost. So instead, I just sat there, watching the house for any signs of movement.

We sat in silence for a few minutes before Loraine spoke. "Christian. What do you think is happening to Rose? I mean, what's it like to change into a vampire and how do you think her being a demon has made things different?"

I wasn't sure how to answer, because honestly, I had no idea. So instead of speculating about Rose's experience, I stuck with what I *did* know.

Loraine's eyes remained glued to mine as I explained the process of vampire creation, but I could see by the look on her face that I hadn't really answered her question, so I added, "It doesn't hurt, Loraine."

The small smile that crept across her sad face told me she wasn't convinced. I'm sure that watching her daughter rise as a vampire and then drift dark wasn't an easy thing to process, but I didn't know what else to say to convince her that everything would be all right. I thought about telling her the rest of the story, about how when a new Sire turns their first vampire that they were actually choosing their consort. But I didn't think the idea of Rose's and my life being connected to the point of dying if the other one does, was something Loraine needed to be reminded of right now. Besides, as I looked out the window into the park, I noticed all the people had finally left.

"I'm going to check out the park, I'll be right back. Do you want to go with me or stay here?" I asked.

"I'll stay here, I guess. But if you stop thinking about Rose or me, I'll most likely disappear. If that happens, just call me back when you need me again."

I was pretty sure this was Loraine's way of saying that she needed to get away from the situation. I figured the oblivion that she faded away to would be a good break for her. As I made my way out of the car and into the park, I purposely guarded my thoughts. As I approached the bridge I looked back and noticed she was gone. I hoped she would find some peace, if only for a little while.

Regaining my focus, I continued to walk into the park. I could smell the blood before I even reached the bridge. I caught Rose's scent but it wasn't her blood that was drifting in the air, so that was a good sign. But unfortunately it wasn't Meredith's either. I would have recognized the sharp tinge of her blood, since I'd gotten a good whiff when we'd left her bleeding on the floor of Rose's former home all those months ago. No, this wasn't Meredith's blood, just some random human's, which meant Rose had fed.

I was happy to know that Rose was safe, but unfortunately I could also tell that she wasn't anywhere in the vicinity. Our bond would have told me if she was, but instead, it still felt stretched, as if a great distance separated us. I took a deep breath, trying to hold it together. Even though Rose was long gone, I still needed to check to see if Meredith was alive or not. Maybe Rose had truly solved all of our problems within the first few hours of being the hybrid. One could only hope.

I left the dark tunnel under the bridge and flew across the street to hide in the bushes nearest Jeremy and Meredith's brownstone. I listened for any movement or bits of conversation, but what I heard made absolutely no sense.

I picked up on the rustling of sheets, as if someone was climbing into bed, then Jeremy's voice rang out. "I'm so excited we're having a baby, Meredith. Becoming a dad is something I've always wanted."

What the hell? Um...Jeremy was a dad...had been for twenty-one years. I continued to listen, trying to gain some inkling of understanding.

"I'm excited too, honey. I can't wait to be parents for the first time. I've always wanted a baby, and for it to be with you...my dreams have come true."

I listened as they shared a quick kiss, then Jeremy continued. "I feel the same way. I just hope I'll know what I'm doing and will be a good father."

Okay...this was fucked. I tried to think of why in the world Jeremy would be acting as if Rose never existed. I instantly knew that Rose was right, and Meredith had "tricked" Jeremy into staying with her. *Dammit!* This situation just went from bad to worse. Meredith had erased Rose from Jeremy's mind all together.

If Rose came here to confront Meredith and save her dad, only to realize that her father had no clue who she was, I could only imagine the devastation she must have felt. If she was dark before, there was no telling what she'd be like now. The negative emotions caused by knowing your father—your *only* living family—had just been forced to forget who you were...*Oh man.* I was surprised that Rose hadn't ripped off Meredith's head right then and there. Then again, what if Meredith wasn't here when Rose approached her dad? What if Jeremy turned her away, not knowing who she was? The picture I now imagined was one of Rose running off into the night, crying from a broken heart.

Dread settled in my chest as I flew from the bushes and back to the car. There was no reason for me to stay here any longer. I couldn't confront Meredith by myself and I couldn't approach Jeremy either, because most likely, he wouldn't have any clue as to who I was. I eased away from the curb, gunning it once I was around the block. I had to get back to The Rising Pit and tell Evie everything that had happened.

On the way back to Seela, I tried to concentrate and force my powers into revealing where Rose was, but it just wasn't working. Frustrated, I tried to think back through every conversation we'd ever shared, hoping to spark a clue as to where she could have gone. It would have been nice if I'd been able to read her thoughts before I changed her, or if Evie had been able to scan her at some point, but unfortunately that never happened either. I almost laughed out loud at our ignorance. Originally, I had thought we couldn't scan Rose because she was purposely guarding her thoughts from us, but in reality, it was because she was a demon.

Demons, or zôts, were something that none of us had ever encountered until the situation with Rose and Meredith had developed. Balam, Evie's Sire, had been helpful with his information, but this was also a first for the elders as well. Throughout the centuries it was thought that whenever a vampire drifted dark, it was a random event brought on by embracing their darkness that led to them reveling in the kill. Who knew that the real reason was because they had accidentally fed from a demon? Our clan had experienced all this when Terrance was infected by Meredith. But luckily, he'd fallen in love with Loraine and became the only vampire in existence to come out of it alive. It had been Loraine's calming ability that allowed Terrance to retain a hint of lightness in his soul, and that was the *only* reason we ended up not having to kill him.

Now with Rose running around with a broken heart, I had no idea what we were supposed to do next. She was the only weapon that could destroy Meredith and we had—*I had*, just lost her. *Can you say cluster-fuck?*

I could only imagine how dark I'd drifted with all these thoughts running through my head. So when I pulled into the parking lot of The Rising Pit, I turned off the car, closed my eyes, and took a few deep breaths to calm myself. The news I had for Evie and the clan wasn't going to make them happy and I didn't want to add to their stress by showing up looking even more out of control.

My meditative efforts were interrupted when Terrance knocked on the window of my car. I opened the door and stepped out, praying he didn't have more bad news.

"What's up?"

"I heard you pull up. So, what'd you find out?"

While I wasn't surprised by his question, I *was* confused as to why he'd left the club to ask me alone. I wondered what other factors had motivated this one-on-one meeting. I scanned Terrance's thoughts and found out exactly why he was here. He was trying to warn me.

Apparently as soon as I left, Evie and Dax had discussed the situation with the rest of the clan. The outcome was that if

I was unable to get Rose back safely, or if when I did bring her back she was dark and out of control, they were going to have to consider the possibility of putting an end to her, which would of course in turn, kill me as well.

I tried to show no reaction but fell back against the side of my car for support. I couldn't believe that Evie would contemplate killing Rose and therefore me, or that she was second guessing the decisions I'd made. But, it was the fact that I was now considering getting in my car and leaving my family behind that bothered me the most. I hated the idea of them being unprotected, but honestly, what did my presence do for them right now? Nothing. We would all remain sitting ducks until I got Rose back and we found out whether or not she was really meant to be our salvation. Continuing to search for Rose on my own was the only choice.

"Terrance, just tell them that I know what I'm doing, and I'll be back soon."

He nodded, and I could tell by the look in his eyes that he was well aware that I'd scanned his thoughts. He clapped me on the back as I turned toward my car. "Just be careful, man. You're going to have to figure out a way to get some blood bags to keep with you, so you don't risk feeding off any demons Meredith has in the area."

"Thank you, and don't worry, I'll be fine."

The last thing I saw as I drove away from my home and the family I'd spent over six hundred years with, was Terrance raising his hand in goodbye before he reentered the club.

CHAPTER TEN

Freeing

(Rose)

I couldn't believe that I'd ran so far from Masen already.
Having the speed of a vampire and a demon truly made me the
fastest thing alive. Looking around, I wasn't even sure where I
was. I was standing in the center of a wheat field, lined on the
far edge with tall oak and hickory trees. It was still night but I
could tell that the sun would be rising in just a few hours. The
idea that I could sleep whenever and where ever I wanted,
continuing on at my convenience, caused a smile to drift across
my face. I would literally never have to worry about anything
ever again.

I slowed my pace, enjoying the soft glow the yellow wheat
gave off in the moonlight. My hand brushed the tops of the
stalks as I walked toward the small forest. I could make out
lights in the distance and figured it'd make as good a place as
any to stop and feed. I didn't have any real direction that I

wanted to head, so the idea of starting my world-wide tour in the next town seemed like the most obvious thing to do. Who knew where it would lead me. Maybe I would stay for a few days and get to know the locals, or maybe I would book a flight and head overseas to check out London and Tuscany like I'd always dreamt of.

I came to the edge of town in a matter of seconds. I glanced at the highway sign and found that I was in Mt. Vernon, a small town outside of Springfield, Missouri.

Okay, maybe I would just feed and catch a few hours sleep and move onto somewhere else. From every history lesson I could remember, besides Missouri being the 24th state admitted to the Union, and the birthplace of Harry Truman, I didn't recall anything else about Missouri that would be considered *amazing*.

Oh wait! Yes, I did. Missouri was where Samuel Clemens, writing as Mark Twain, penned *The Adventures of Tom Sawyer* and its sequel, *Adventures of Huckleberry Finn*. Little did people know that the story was set around his real life in Hannibal, Missouri, including the caves where Indian, or Injun Joe had hid; they—

and many other details from his books—were real and could be

toured to this very day. Excited by my recollection, I was

suddenly consumed by the idea of checking out and possibly

hiding in these exact caves.

I stumbled at the thought...*Hide? Why in the world would I*

need to hide? The emotions warring inside my mind were making

me dizzy. Literally, I felt like I was weaving on my feet. I didn't

think I needed to feed again, but one minute I was fine and

fearless, and the next I felt paranoid and wracked with fear.

I made my way into town, using the shadows of the old

buildings to conceal my movements. Mt. Vernon had a

historical feel that seemed antiquated until you looked closer; in

reality, it was just really old. No businesses were open, and no

one was out walking to provide me with an easy meal so I

decided to find a place to sleep; I would just wait until the town

woke and feed in the morning instead.

I raced through the dark streets, looking for the perfect

place to spend the night. Finally, I saw a lumber mill at the end of the street. It looked promising and would provide plenty of

places to hide. I leapt high into the rafters and curled up into a

ball behind the large stores of wood and welcomed the oblivion

of sleep. Too bad, all I got were nightmares instead.

Nightmares of stone and blood, demons and vampires, humans

and death. I felt myself connecting to every aspect of these

disturbing scenes as if I was the main character in each role: the

human girl being sacrificed, the demon queen delivering the

killing blow, the vampire princess drinking the blood. The

images swirled and melded together and then I was staring at a

replica of myself flying up into the air. A scary-ass replica. I had

dark hair and crimson eyes, much as I did now, but instead of

my fangs being pointed and dainty, they were jagged razors,

extending past my lower lips, but that wasn't the worst part.

The thing that freaked me out the most were the black wings

that had sprouted from my back.

Jolting upright I quickly leapt into a defensive stance. I

knew within seconds no one was actually attacking me, but as I settled back to sleep, I couldn't shake the feeling there was now something out there that I should fear.

$$* * * * *$$

(Christian)

As I pulled onto the highway, I had no idea which way to go. Rose could have run north and already be in Canada, or maybe to the west and was hanging out in Arizona by now. But the one thing I did know was that Terrance was right; I needed to stock up on blood bags for my trip, and with the sun approaching in just a few hours, it was imperative I find somewhere safe to sleep.

While the sun didn't burn us, once it rose we were rendered comatose and wouldn't rise again until it set. If I were to remain somewhere in the open and be discovered, I'm sure I'd wake up in the morgue, as I would appear dead to anyone who found me. That was why all vampire clans maintained a secure lair, usually below ground, as a way to guarantee their safety.

As I drove toward the nearest hospital, I thought about The Rising Pit and our lair deep beneath it. It had been the perfect cover for our family. We all worked in the club at night and retired to the pit below before morning. It was going to be weird not waking up in my own bed for the first time in years.

It only took a few minutes on the freeway before I came to the exit that would lead me to the hospital. Turning into the parking lot of St. Mary's Regional, I was suddenly hit with an idea. If Rose was really as bad as everyone thought, maybe I would just have to watch the news and look for an increased number of injuries or deaths due to attacks and massive blood loss to find out where she was. While I wanted to smile at the fact that I now had a semi-decent plan to follow, the idea of Rose killing and hurting people wiped the thought from my mind. How could I smile when the love of my life, the woman I'd longed to spend eternity with, was now lost to me and probably losing herself more and more with each passing minute?

I exited the car and walked toward the emergency entrance. I hoped that there weren't very many people in need of medical care this evening, because I really didn't want to have to waste time biting and using my sedative to erase my appearance here tonight from everyone's mind.

Luckily, the nurse behind the counter was preoccupied with the elderly man who seemed to be complaining of chest pains. I used the distraction to fly through the nearby door and search for the hospital's blood bank. It only took seconds before I found the refrigerated room. I quickly grabbed a large self-cooling container and quickly filled it with bags; I didn't care what the blood type was. I felt bad about taking any of it, but I especially didn't want to take just one type, leaving them depleted for those in need of that particular kind.

I hadn't run into anyone, since to most I was just a breeze of wind, but as I got back in my car, I wondered if there had been any cameras in the blood bank that I should have taken out. Unfortunately, I didn't have time to worry about it and I figured if anyone did try to come after me, I would just have to risk biting them and erase the memory of why they were there.

I turned back onto the highway and tried to think of a safe place to sleep for the night, when suddenly my claircognizance flared to life. I instantly knew exactly where to go. Jillian's.

Rose's best friend might have some ideas of where Rose would have fled to. Plus, somehow I knew that I'd be safe staying in her home for the night. I took the next exit and quickly found my way to Jillian's house. Her car was in the driveway and there was only one light on in the upstairs window. It was close to morning, so I wasn't sure if she had stayed up late or if she was an early riser. Either way, I knew this was exactly where I needed to be, but was still unsure why.

I parked across the street and quickly drained two blood bags before transferring the cooler to the trunk of my car. I wouldn't need any more blood until after I rose tomorrow night.

Walking across the street and up to Jillian's front door had me on edge. I wasn't sure exactly what to say, or if I would be forced to have some sort of confrontation with her parents, but luckily, when I knocked on the door, Jillian opened it with a smile on her face.

"Hi, Christian. I wondered how long it would take you to show up."

CHAPTER ELEVEN

Funeral

(Meredith)

After hanging up with the realtor, I realized it was almost time for me to head to Damien's funeral. As anxious as I was to start the search for our new home, I simply couldn't miss the opportunity to talk to Raúl. If I got him to take over where Damien left off, we'd be back on track in creating my army within the week.

Jeremy had already left for work after a morning of utter bliss. We'd made love after waking, both excited about the new prospects for our future. It was a good day. I'd thought about introducing some human blood to Jeremy as well, to kick start his immortal genes, but I couldn't risk mixing it with mine in case it affected our mind bond in some unexpected way. So for now, he'd just have to remain the clueless demon man I loved.

As I pulled out of the driveway, I took an extra moment to look back at my house. My happiness faded slightly at the thought of leaving my home permanently. Like Jeremy had pointed out, I had lived here for such a long time. But it wasn't the idea of moving somewhere else that was upsetting to me, but instead, the fact that I was being forced to do so by a bunch of vampires who wanted me dead. To say it pissed me off was putting it mildly. I'd always thought of becoming immortal and creating my army as a defensive maneuver, but now, with the "message" they had left me in the park, maybe my efforts would need to become more offensive instead.

As I pulled into the funeral home's parking lot, I continued to contemplate what a change of plans like that would mean exactly. I'd always thought I'd just hole up and be prepared in case they came after me, but now...it looked like planning an attack may have to be my next move.

"Hello, Meredith. Thank you so much for coming." Thankfully Raúl was the first one to greet me as I walked through the white double doors. It wasn't that I felt uncomfortable being here, but just that I hadn't really had any interaction with Damien's extended family besides seeing them at our demon meetings.

"Of course, Raúl. It's just so horrible what happened."

The slight tilt to his head made me nervous. Raúl and a few select others were very aware of what Damien and I had been doing, and suddenly I worried that maybe they'd put two and two together and figured out that it was me who'd killed their cousin.

"He'd be so pleased you came. I know he had developed some pretty strong feelings for you."

All I could do was nod my head and clasp his hand. I had no idea that Damien had shared his "feelings" for me with anyone else. I wasn't comfortable with the idea of him talking about me to other people, which meant talking to Raúl later had yet another purpose. I had to find out what all Damien had told them.

"Will there be a wake afterwards?"

"Yes, actually, it's in the same place where we held our meetings. My mother thought it was fitting, as he was truly responsible for bringing us all together. We'd all be pleased if you'd join us; we have a pretty big surprise to share with you."

Shit. I did not like surprises.

"Of course, I'll be there."

I sat through Damien's funeral, listening to sobs and prayers. So far, nothing was being said by the priest or family members that sounded like they thought I was to blame, but who knew? Maybe they were holding back to keep up appearances for the non-demon attendees. I started getting nervous that once we arrived at the meeting site they'd all end up turning on me. As anxiety filled my thoughts, I decided I'd have to find a human to drink from on the drive to the wake. That way, if they did try anything, I'd be freshly juiced and unstoppable. No one had been drinking blood as long as I had, and therefore, wouldn't even come close to my strength or speed. I hoped that I didn't have to fight Damien's family, but if I was forced to...I would.

As the funeral came to an end, I made sure to catch Raúl before heading out to my car. "That was a beautiful service. Are you headed straight to the wake?"

"Yes, I have to help clear and transport all the flower arrangements, but I'll be there soon."

I smiled and tried to gauge his reactions. "All right, is there anything I can do to help?"

"Yes, actually, we could use some cups."

"No problem, I'll stop and pick some up then meet you there." This gave me the perfect excuse to delay my trip and feed.

As I left the local Wal-Mart, I saw a hitchhiker standing on the corner. I picked him up, and after a few blocks and a quick stop behind the nearest garbage dumpster, I'd quenched my thirst and was on my way again to the meeting facility. His blood was a boost to my system, one that amped up my strength and eliminated my fears. I knew if anyone tried to hurt me, they would be in for a big surprise.

Once I arrived, I made my way inside and placed the cups on the empty table. I was used to being the leader of the meetings here, but today, until I could figure out exactly what was going on, I decided to lay low and took a seat in the far corner. I watched everyone mill around, exchanging hugs and stories about Damien, until finally Raúl and the last few members of his family came through the door.

After placing the flower arrangements and a few odds and ends around the room, Raúl's mother stepped to the front to gain everyone's attention. "*A-hem.* I'd like to thank you all for coming today. The service was beautiful and I appreciate all the kind words you had to say about my nephew. But now, I have some important words of my own to share. As most of you know, Damien's death was no accident."

Oh shit! I tensed up. If I was going to be hung out to dry, this was the moment.

"But his death did give our family an opportunity to learn things we didn't know, gain an understanding of our past, and provide a new course for our future."

What's with the damn riddles? I watched as Raúl and his cousins set the table with food platters and a large punch bowl, as I continued to listen to his mom.

"Damien was killed by vampires, and now we have a chance to learn from our ancestors and gain enough strength and power to exact our revenge."

My mouth almost hit the floor. I sat in stunned silence as I watched Raúl mix blood with the punch, just like I'd done the last time we were here. I stared as everyone grabbed one of the cups I'd brought and dip them into the blood laced concoction. They all stood around shaking their heads and bobbing back and forth on their feet like they were a bunch of prize fighters preparing for their big bout.

Raúl caught my eye, and made his way over to me. "See, I told you you'd be surprised."

"Um...you could say that again. What's going on? Who told them about the vampires and how'd you convince them to start drinking blood?"

"I did. When the police found Damien's body, it was me and my mom who went to identify him. When I saw his neck had been bitten and shredded like that, I knew it was the vampires you told us about. I decided to tell my mom and that we'd been drinking blood in an effort to get stronger and become immortal like our ancestors. As she stood there looking at Damien and listening to the story, I saw something change inside her. Once we left, she said that she was going to bring everyone on board so we could get revenge for Damien's death and help protect you in the process. She got the family together that same night and relayed everything I had told her and now...here we are. Everyone is ready to help you take on the vampires."

The amount of twisted joy I felt was unexplainable. I couldn't believe that by killing the one person who'd threatened me, I had just created a willing army in a matter of days. Everyone here was gaining strength in a controlled manner by ingesting blood in smaller amounts, which meant I wouldn't have to worry about being challenged again. This was perfect! The idea that Damien was killed by the vampires gave me a room full of demons with the motivation to do anything I asked, and I was so pleased that I wouldn't have to hide or trick them into drinking the blood to do so. We could now openly plan our attack and discuss our experiences together. Raúl was

right, this was a big surprise...but one I didn't mind at all.

CHAPTER TWELVE

Complete Shock

(Christian)

I wasn't sure what Jillian meant, or why it looked like she was expecting me, but I headed inside, hoping to find out why my psychic gift had led me to her doorstep.

"Thank you," I said as I crossed the threshold. "You don't seem very surprised to see me after all this time, Jillian. Can I ask why that is?" I wasn't sure if confronting her right away was a good idea or not, but it was the path my mind was telling me to take so I went with it.

She talked over her shoulder as we walked into the dark kitchen. "I'm not surprised to see you, Christian. I texted you to come over as soon as you could. Oh, and by the way, my parents are in Brazil on vacation to check out the place I'll *supposedly* be living in next year, so we have the house to ourselves."

I grabbed my phone and checked for the message I'd apparently missed. Yep, sure enough, there was her text. It struck me as odd that Jillian would be texting me at all, or why she seemed to understand that we needed to be alone, and I also didn't get what she meant by "supposedly living in." To say I was confused was a huge understatement.

"Have you heard from Rose recently?" I decided to not try and decipher her statements and got to the real reason I thought I was here. I hoped Rose had once again reached out to her best friend and that Jillian could therefore provide me a direction to head in my search. What I got instead was a complete shock.

"No, but William said that Justin and I can help you look for her."

I spun around so fast that I knocked the bar stool over. Jillian was standing next to the refrigerator with a blood bag to her lips. "Want some?"

"Holy shit, Jillian! You're a vampire?"

"Took you long enough." She smiled and shrugged her shoulders. "After you and Rose disappeared all those months ago, Justin and I continued to see each other. It didn't take long before we really did fall in love. After I graduated college, he petitioned William to change me and then explained what was up. I, of course, jumped at the chance to be with him forever."

"How long? And do you know everything that's happened with Rose and our clan?" I assumed she did, since she was drinking from a bag.

"Yes and no. I've been a vampire for just a few weeks, but it was only earlier tonight that Evie contacted our Sire to explain about the demon situation. That's also when she told us about Rose, and how by becoming the hybrid, that she was now our only hope in stopping them."

She took another sip from the bag, then hopped up onto the counter. "I can't say that I wasn't ticked to find out that not only was my best friend a frickin' demon, but now some crazy ass cross-breed hybrid. But I was happy when William agreed to let us go with you, since after all, I *have* been her best friend for years. Evangeline told us that you'd gone looking for her and agreed that maybe I could be of some help."

I couldn't process everything that had happened in such a short span of time. Jillian turned into a vampire, Rose missing, Evie contacting another clan to aid in our cause. It was so much to take in. But thinking about all Rose and I had been caught up in, it wasn't a surprise that I'd missed so much of what had happened outside our own little world. I suppose it shouldn't be shocking that Justin and Jillian had continued seeing each other, or that he'd petitioned to have her turned. But, I couldn't deny that I felt a little pissed off that Evie had gone to their clan behind my back. I was the new Sire now, and that should have been something I'd decided to do, not her. Then again, after what I'd learned from Terrance, I supposed I should have expected it. If Evie felt that they would eventually have to take a stand against Rose and me, she'd want to have her backup lined up. *Wow. What a fucked up mess.*

"Well, I guess I should be grateful that you and Justin will be joining me, but back to my original question...has Rose contacted you again? Do you know where we should be looking for her?"

"No. That's the part that I have no clue about. I haven't heard from her since she threatened to kill me." Her fake giggle told me that she too was upset about everything that had transpired.

I didn't know what she was talking about, so I assumed it was just one more secret that Rose had decided to keep from me. Shaking my head, I suddenly felt a tug in my chest as a tremor swept over my body. Our bond was wearing thinner and thinner by the hour, and right now I was starting to feel the effects. If Jillian could help in any way to find Rose sooner rather than later, I would be grateful for her assistance.

"You said that your parents are on vacation and we have the house to ourselves, right?"

"Yes, I used my sedative to convince them that I'd be living in Brazil to play for their volleyball team. They're ranked second in the world, you know."

"No, I didn't know that, but does that mean that we can sleep here, uninterrupted for the day?"

"Yes. Exactly. Justin is gathering more blood bags for our trip, and will join us here tomorrow once the sun goes down. Now, let me show you to the guest room."

I followed Jillian down the hall to a nice room with simple furnishings. The blinds were already pulled, so I thanked her and fell straight into the comfortable bed. My head was spinning from everything I'd just learned, and the emotions it was causing within me, had me drifting as I settled in. As much as I wanted to flesh out the next step of our plan, it was something I'd have to process tomorrow because for the first time in hundreds of years, I was actually feeling tired.

CHAPTER THIRTEEN

Faith

(Evie)

After my meeting with William, the Sire of the closest clan, I rode back to The Rising Pit in the passenger seat of Dax's SUV. I sat in silence because I couldn't help feeling guilty. I knew it was Christian's place to reach out as the new Sire, but with him in search of Rose, and the possibility of them both turning dark in this process, I felt like I'd been left with no choice. He hadn't returned from his search and honestly, I didn't have a clue if he ever would. Therefore, as the clan's *original* Sire, their safety would always be my responsibility and main priority.

Dax didn't say a word as we pulled up to the club. Not wanting oversensitive ears to hear my concerns, I remained in the car and turned to him. "I don't know what else to do, Dax. I'm not sure if I should call Balam and tell him that we had a hybrid, but lost her; or that we have a new Sire in the clan, but that he too is now drifted dark and gone; or if I should just shut this place down and move everyone to somewhere safe."

He took my hands in his and looked into my eyes. "Where would we go, Evie? Where *is* somewhere safe? We now know demons litter the world because of the few cases of vampires drifting dark, so what makes you think that no matter where we'd move, we wouldn't run into another hive of them?"

I dropped my head into my hands, realizing he was right. There wasn't anywhere we could go that demons wouldn't be a concern. It's just that here, they weren't something that we'd accidentally run into, but instead were a direct threat to our existence. Meredith was creating an army to come after us, and if we didn't get Rose and Christian back soon, I had no idea what we'd do. It was the reason that I'd agreed to let Justin and Jillian go with Christian to help look for her. I wasn't sure about it at first, but when they'd explained that Jillian had been Rose's best friend for years, I thought that maybe she could be of some assistance, so I gave them Christian's cell number and hoped they could meet up soon.

"Let's go inside, honey. The sun's almost up and maybe by tomorrow night Christian will have found her and all this will be behind us." Dax flew from the truck and had my door open within seconds. "Besides, if we just keep an eye on Meredith and her demon meetings, we should get the jump on anything she has planned."

He was right. I could send Renard and Loni back to keep tabs on her and her meetings. It'd take a little time to set up though, since I'd have to secure a place for them to sleep during the day without being interrupted. Hotels were fine once in a while, but after you stayed too long, people began to question a vampire's odd hours. No, I'd have to make sure they'd be safe, and then I'd send them on an extended stakeout until this mess was over.

"You're right. I guess that's all we can really do until Rose and Christian return."

We walked back into the club, hand and hand. Dax had always been my rock. He was my consort and the man I would love forever. As we made our way down the spiral staircase into the pit, sealing the circular stage over our heads, I tried to imagine what Christian must be going through. To have woken up and instantly been forced to function without his consort; losing her before even having a single moment to bask in the joy of being together forever...I shook my head, feeling a tear slide down my cheek as we entered our room.

"I don't think I can hurt him, Dax. If Christian truly turns dark because of all this, I don't think I can deliver the true death. He's been my son for hundreds of years and is the most kind hearted person I've ever known."

Dax embraced me as we lay down. "Have faith, Evie. Christian turned Rose feeling it was the right thing to do. We just have to trust him."

I let his words soak into my heart as I fell comatose for the day.

* * * * *

(Rose)

I looked around the now illuminated lumber mill. Morning

had come, but the nightmares I'd experienced left me feeling

trapped and scared. I took a deep breath and eased out of my

hiding place. No one was here now, but I knew it wouldn't be

long before workers started to arrive to begin their day.

I figured that feeding here would be a good idea, as long as

there weren't too many people that showed up at once. Luckily,

the supervisor was the first one on site. I watched from my

perch as he unlocked the gate and then the office doors. A few

minutes later, he wandered out into the open space and I made

my move.

Leaping down from the ceiling, I landed directly behind

him and sunk my fangs into his neck before he could even turn

around. I tried to use my sedative again and program it so he

wouldn't feel pain or remember anything, but just like before,

the euphoria his blood sparked within me had my mind

drifting, causing me to lose all focus until he was lying motionless on the sawdust covered ground.

I watched as his blood pooled, mixing with the tiny wood flakes. The pattern it made was amusing and I found myself reaching out to draw pictures in it. The consistency reminded me of the finger paints I used in grade school, but before I could finish drawing my smiley face, I heard cars pulling up outside. I was gone in seconds and almost to the edge of town before I remembered I needed a map. I stopped at the gas station next to the freeway and casually walked in and paid for the small atlas with the change I had in my pockets. Once I made sure I was headed in the correct direction, I set off for the caves again. A smile crept across my face at the thought of the underground caverns. For reasons I didn't understand, I simply couldn't wait to get there.

CHAPTER FOURTEEN

Wrong

(Meredith)

After Raúl's revelation, I mingled and talked to all of his family, especially his mother, Lupé. She was stern but had an excited edge to her, probably due to the affects of the human blood. She told me that even though she was sad about losing Damien, she was happy to be out of the dark and felt that this new way of life for her family was something the gods wanted to happen.

I wasn't sure about that, but it was certainly something that *I* wanted to happen. She had suggested that we move the meeting to her house, since it was further from the city and wouldn't draw attention. We'd be needing more and more blood, so being more secluded while we continued to grow stronger and make our plans sounded like a great idea to me. I thanked her and announced that next week's meeting would be held at her house.

As I drove home I couldn't help feeling giddy. When I'd left the wake, everyone had still been talking about how the blood had started to give them speed and strength. Some had even started demonstrating by lifting their relatives high into the air, and others just raced around chasing one another in an endless game of tag. It was like watching children and it brought joy to my heart. My race...demons thriving in the twenty-first century. Who could have guessed it? But as I pulled into my driveway, I thought about my grandmother's words, *"I can tell that you are changing, and I'm afraid that what you've started will not be good for our race."*

I could only hope that she was wrong.

* * * * *

(Christian)

The last thing a vampire thought of before falling comatose was also the first thing they'd think of upon waking. I'd spent the last year making it a habit to think of Rose before

I fell asleep. However, as I woke in Jillian's guest room, it wasn't the usual image of me embracing Rose that greeted me; instead, it was one of me running after her.

I supposed it only made sense, since that's literally what I was doing; chasing after my consort in an effort to save her and myself. As much as I didn't want to admit it, I could feel that I was losing her. Our bond was stretched so thin that it was making me weak. I was pretty sure if she continued to drift dark it would be as effective in killing me as if she'd actually died.

After straightening the guest room I left the house and walked out to my car. I couldn't bear to think of anything happening to Rose without it sending me into a depressive spiral. I needed to get a hold of myself before Jillian and Justin saw that I'd drifted dark again and reported it back to their Sire. I was sure if Evie found out that I hadn't returned to my normal coloring yet, she'd assume the worst, and then not only would I be racing to find Rose, I'd be running for my life as well.

I grabbed a couple blood bags from the trunk and sat in my front seat, trying to gain some small measure of control. The blood helped, but as I imagined Rose out feeding on her own, killing more innocent people, I knew I was far from okay. I had no idea what I was going to do if once I found her, she really *was* bad. I'd never heard of any Sire having to abandon their chosen consort in all of our vampire history, not that I could imagine doing so even if it was a possibility. No, walking away was never an option; instead it always came back to the both of us meeting the true death. I almost threw up at the thought.

I closed my eyes and tried to recall the last time Rose and I had been really happy together. I thought it was when she'd been hiding out with me after her attack on Meredith, but in hindsight I was wrong. She'd been struggling to keep her demon side a secret and had been purposely pushing me away in an attempt to keep me safe. I thought back to when she'd told me she knew I was a vampire and agreed to be my consort, but even then, it was after she'd lost her father thanks again to

Meredith. I guess the last time we'd been truly happy was when I'd been in the dark about Rose knowing my secret. We'd dated like a normal couple and had genuinely fallen in love.

A sharp wrap on my window pulled me out of my current reverie.

"Hey, come back inside so we can work out a plan, okay?" Justin's face was serious but didn't show signs of worry or fear, so I assumed my coloring had drifted back to normal.

I joined him and Jillian in the kitchen and sat quietly as they drank their evening meal.

"So, do you have any idea where Rose could be right now?" Jillian asked.

My first instinct was to get defensive, but I knew it wouldn't help. "No. I have no idea. She went to Masen and I tracked her to her dad's house but she was gone by the time I arrived. Do you have any thoughts?" I scoffed.

"Not really. I mean as kids we usually just hung around here or Masen, since both of our parents worked all the time. We didn't really ever take vacations and if we did, it was only to places like Disneyland or Six Flags. I can't really see her going there, though, 'cause she used to say that all that cheery, happy go lucky shit drove her crazy."

Well, great. The room fell silent as we all realized we didn't have a clue where to start. It was already looking like this was going to be a complete waste of time. Time I didn't have.

Jillian's voice interrupted my depressive thoughts. "Are you sure she left Masen? Maybe she was just feeding and hiding out until she could go back and finish off Meredith."

Her question made sense, but I also had to trust my instincts. "No. I can feel that she's gone. Our bond has grown really weak, as if it's being stretched by a large distance."

I hated admitting it, but what would be the point of keeping anything from them. Jillian was her friend and Justin had been the one to help her understand everything when Terrance had lied to her. They would help me if they could.

Just then, I got a lucky break. Loraine appeared above me, but for no more than six or seven seconds. In my mind I heard her say, *"Caves, Christian. You have to start looking in caves."*

She was gone before I could ask a question of my own, and no matter how much I thought about her or Rose, she didn't reappear. I didn't understand where Loraine went when she disappeared from our world, but the fact that I couldn't reach her now had me extremely concerned.

"What's wrong? You've started drifting again," Justin stated.

I didn't have time to explain about Loraine. "I have an idea of where we need to go. Where is the nearest set of caves to here?"

Jillian looked at me with a raised eyebrow, then headed straight to the computer in her father's study. After a quick internet search, we knew the three closest set of caves were in Virginia, Kentucky, and Missouri.

As worried as I was about Loraine, I knew it would do me no good to dwell on it. Plus, her clue about Rose was the first thing I had to go on and I wasn't about to waste it. I wanted us to all break up and each take one location, but Justin suggested we remain together in case one of them found her first. He thought I needed to be there, wherever we found her. The instant he said it I knew he was right. The certainty of knowing I would see Rose again made me happy, but the idea that she could hurt her friends if I wasn't there to stop her left me unsettled.

I forced myself to stop analyzing the situation and focused on our plan to get moving. I had to find Rose quickly and we'd be a lot faster on foot. So, after packing our supplies, we all sprinted towards Virginia, hoping for a lucky break.

* * * * *

(Loraine)

Blood, wings, bats, caves, Rose—Blood, wings, bats, caves, Rose. It was the nightmare I'd been stuck in since I'd disappeared from Christian's car. I'd hoped for some relief from this god-awful situation when Christian had left me sitting there alone. But instead of falling into oblivion like every other time I'd left the earthly plane, I'd been thrown straight into this reoccurring nightmare.

I could see tall stone temples and people in tribal clothing everywhere I looked. There were flashes of human sacrifices and a winged creature. I had no idea what I was seeing or when it was taking place, but the main focus I kept getting pulled back to were the images being drawn on cave walls. So when I'd felt myself being pulled back into my corporeal form, I knew that was the message I needed to deliver.

I found Christian in the kitchen of Rose's best friend, Jillian. As always, I immediately received the information I needed; Jillian was now a vampire and was here with her boyfriend, Justin, in an effort to help find Rose.

As soon as Christian spotted me, I had already begun to fade and knew I better talk fast. *"Caves, Christian. You have to start looking in caves."*

I was gone a second later, once again pulled back and being forced to witness this gruesome scene. It had changed slightly and was now focused on the winged creature. The thing was obviously female and had long black hair and sharp jagged teeth. The fear that radiated from the village it flew over was palpable. I could literally feel the terror of those poor people, and for the first time, I was happy I was already dead.

I was forced to watch as this beast annihilated an entire village, slaughtering men, women, and children. Their screams pierced my mind and all I could do was cry. Village after village was decimated, and the monster grew more vile with each and every kill. It seemed as if the horror would never stop, and then suddenly it was over. For everyone. The next image I got was of an entire continent completely devastated. I knew then that I'd just witnessed an entire race being wiped from existence.

The scene started to clear and I found myself finally fading into the oblivion I'd longed for. I tried to concentrate and piece together how any of this could be connected to Rose and Christian, but my mind was too fragile from all I'd seen to make any sense of it. My body started to shake as I thought about that horrible creature hurting my baby. I couldn't understand why I'd been forced to see something like this, and could only hope that somehow it was leading me to some helpful information. I had to hold onto the hope that something good would come out of this, because if the death and destruction I saw here had anything to do with our future, I never wanted to return.

With an overwhelming sense of doom, I simply closed my eyes and let the darkness swallow me whole.

CHAPTER FIFTEEN

New View

(Meredith)

Today was the day Jeremy and I were starting the search for our new home. Since everything was in order with Raúl and his family, I was excited to shift my focus to something else besides death and blood.

"Babe. You ready to go? The realtor will be here in just a few minutes," Jeremy called out.

"Yes, honey. I'm ready. You sound excited. Does she have some good prospects for us to look at today?"

"Actually, yes. I never thought house hunting would be something I'd enjoy doing again after all these years, but I know a couple of the places have fantastic views and I'm interested to see if she's managed to get everything on our wish list."

A fantastic new view was just what I needed, because every time I looked out the window of the living room or our upstairs bedroom, I looked straight into the park and was reminded of why we needed to move. It was imperative that I get somewhere new and hide from Christian's vampire clan while my army continued to grow. We weren't ready to take them on just yet, but it wouldn't be too long before we were.

"Hey, Mer? Can you come here for a second?" Jeremy's voice had lost its cheerful tone, so I headed upstairs to see what he needed. As I rounded the corner of our bedroom I found him standing next to his dresser, holding an old tattered wallet.

"I've been having trouble with this drawer and just figured out the reason why. This old thing was stuck behind it. Do you know who this girl is?"

He was staring at a picture of Rose. *Son of a bitch!* I'd forgotten all about this wallet. He had told me months ago that he'd lost it so I'd simply bought him a new one and replaced all his cards and photos, which of course I removed after feeding him my blood and erasing Rose from his mind.

"I'm not sure." I tried not to let my eyes flare or distress seep into my voice.

"Hmm. She looks familiar, but I can't quite place her," he continued.

I wanted to thank the gods when the doorbell rang.

"Well, time to go," he said. Then with a shake of his head, he tossed the wallet onto the top of the dresser and turned to grab his jacket from the end of the bed. "Ready?"

All I could do was nod. I followed him downstairs and grabbed our coffee mugs from the kitchen while he answered the door. Quickly using the small paring knife, I nicked my finger and added a few more drops of my blood to his coffee. Taking a deep breath, I grabbed my purse from the credenza and headed to meet him and our realtor, Cheryl, at the front door.

"Hi, Cheryl. Thank you again for driving us today. We're both very excited," I said.

"You're welcome, Meredith. But I think you're going to have a hard time choosing between the selections I've got lined up for you, so if you're both ready, let's get started. The first one I have to show you is a beautiful single family home on the edge of downtown."

Jeremy locked the house as I headed to the car. I handed him his cup as he joined me, then climbed in the back seat of Cheryl's Mercedes. As I slid across the soft leather seats, I purposely let my skirt ride up and gave Jeremy a quick wink.

I regretted it immediately. He tripped on the curb and dropped his coffee. *Shit!* My little tease was supposed to put him at ease, not cause my problem to go from bad to worse. Now I could only hope my mind bond was strong enough to erase what had just happened in the house, but I wasn't entirely convinced that it was.

As we rode to the first house, I made a plan to excuse myself to the restroom as soon as possible so I could lace my cup instead, but as we pulled up to a stop light, Jeremy reached for my cup. "Do you mind? I'm parched and it is your fault I dropped my coffee," he teased.

I sighed as I watched him drain the remnants of my cup. *So much for that plan.*

I couldn't feed him directly from the vein without causing a horrible mess and mass amounts of hysteria. So, after watching him discard the empty cup in the trash bag located on the floor of Cheryl's car, I simply hoped the house hunting would be enough of a distraction to keep his mind off of Rose's picture.

"What do you think?" Cheryl swept her hand in the direction of the first house, and I wanted to kill her on the spot. It looked almost identical to Jeremy and Loraine's former home. The home they'd spent their entire marriage in, raising their daughter.

Jeremy stood silent and stared at the house for a few moments...a few *excruciating* moments. I was so worried that with the picture of Rose and now looking at a replica of their picture perfect home, that our mind bond would become severed right here on this very spot. I really didn't want to kill Cheryl if I didn't have to, but if Jeremy showed any signs of remembering, I may be left with no other choice.

I touched his shoulder and gently asked, "Should we go in?" His response made me the happiest woman alive.

"No, actually. This isn't at all what I'm looking for. I'm sorry, Cheryl, but can we just move on to the next choice?"

Cheryl nearly tripped over her high heels at Jeremy's request, but after regaining her composure, she simply said, "Of course."

He pulled me close to him once we were in the back seat of the car again. I wasn't sure what thoughts were running through his mind at the moment, but whatever the reason for him not wanting a home like the one he'd had with Loraine, put a smile on my face. Maybe I could trust him to want a future with me without controlling his mind after all. *Ha! Who are you kidding?* It really was laughable. Thinking back to the night Jeremy almost walked out of my life after catching me killing Damien in our garage, yeah...I knew that I still had no choice but to manipulate him. If he were to remember everything I'd done, he'd leave me for sure.

We continued to ride in silence as Cheryl drove us to the next house on her list.

The building was one of the two new glass high-rises, smack dab in the middle of downtown Masen. The three bedroom apartment was located on the twentieth floor and had amazing features. Granite counters, marble fireplaces, vaulted ceilings, and a master suite to die for. Jeremy walked through each room at least three times, then stood in the massive living room, taking it all in. I was staring out the wall of windows, overlooking what felt like the entire city, when he surprised me by asking, "Will this work for you?" I hadn't expected him to like it so much.

"My god, yes of course. It's beautiful."

Turning to Cheryl, he said, "We'll take it. How soon can we move in?"

"Jeremy, wait! We haven't even sold the house yet," I exclaimed. I wasn't sure what had gotten into him.

"We don't need to wait to sell your house, I still have the money from the sale of mine, so we can move in right away." He turned to Cheryl. "Which is something I hope we can do soon."

Cheryl handed him the keys, and pulled the paperwork out of her briefcase. "Of course. Just sign here, and as soon as your deposit check clears tomorrow, the place is yours." She winked, then whispered, "Just one of the benefits of prequalification."

Jeremy took the papers, signed them, then wrote out a check for one-hundred and forty thousand dollars, which was our twenty percent down. "Thank you, Cheryl. Now...let's go celebrate. Lunch is on me."

I was about to ask why he was so gung-ho all of the sudden, but dropped it since moving this quickly only benefited me. We'd be out of the house and safe from the vampires tomorrow and our new home was practically an impenetrable fortress. Plus, I'd get to start decorating our baby's nursery right away, where as in the old house, we would've had to redo an entire room by eliminating the study. Here we had it all. It seemed now the only thing I had to worry about was getting

some of my blood into his meal at lunch to keep this perfect

charade going.

CHAPTER SIXTEEN

Virginia

(Christian)

Before we'd left I'd mapped out our search locations, starting with the closest and working to the furthest away. It only took about two hours for us to reach Virginia and we were now standing outside Luray Caverns.

The caverns had closed hours ago, but thankfully we didn't need lights or permission to get inside. After laying out a plan to explore the entire system and meet back in the specified location, we all broke off to our designated areas. I quickly moved into my section, already knowing we wouldn't find Rose. I didn't mention it because I didn't want to discourage Jillian or Justin, and I certainly didn't want to risk missing something by rushing or being overly confident in my gifts.

As I continued my search I started thinking about Loraine's rushed message. I couldn't understand why we were even searching in caves to begin with. It's not like Rose needed to hide from anyone. If she was using her sedative when she fed, she could simply erase the experience from anyone she bit. But if not, and she was killing people instead, there'd be no reason to worry in that case either—dead people didn't talk. *Hmph...*I thought of Loraine again. *Well...usually, dead people don't talk.*

I tried to focus my thoughts on Loraine and pull her energy to me. I needed her to appear and hopefully provide a little more clarity, but unfortunately, I had no such luck. So instead, I kept stalking through the underground cavern, looking for the woman I loved. I shook my head at the ridiculousness of it. What could a cave possibly have to do with Rose? I knew this was going to be a dead end, but I had to trust Loraine. Wherever she went, or whoever it was that gave her the divine information she always returned with, it was clear that she had access to more information than me, even *with* my gifts.

I continued to contemplate the oddity of our situation as I walked deeper into the caves. Suddenly I found myself in a large open chamber. The "ceiling" was at least thirty feet high, and dome-shaped. As I moved into the area, I ran my hands along the walls while my eyes adjusted. Continuing around the edge, I suddenly noticed that the walls were smoother here, like they'd been worked by hand or worn over by years of water running over them. I didn't see any pools on the ground, and couldn't pick up any sounds of water, so I just kept moving along the wall. I wanted to circle the entire room to get an idea of the overall size, and to see if I could pinpoint a purpose to the space or any tunnels that branched off from it. As I reached the back portion, the surface under my hand changed slightly. It was still smooth but I could sense something else. Squinting hard I could make out ancient drawings that covered the cold stone wall.

The drawings depicted villages and fields of crops with people and animals scattered about. There were also moons and stars and what I assumed were the tribesmen's interpretation of the constellations drawn onto the hard surface. I never expected to find petroglyphs in the caves of

Virginia, which only heightened the joy this discovery brought me. I continued to look at the wide expanse of stone for a few more minutes before I heard Justin shouting my name. I called out and waited for him to find me.

"Whoa!" he exclaimed as he walked into the massive room. "Did you find anything in here?"

"Not really. Just some ancient drawings. How about you? Did you find anything?" I asked, even though I already knew the answer.

"No. I searched my area twice and there wasn't anything or anyone in the whole place."

Jillian walked into the cavern and added her report as well. "I didn't find anything either."

"Well, then let's not waste any more time. We have seven more sets of caves here in Virginia to check, so let's just go." I took one last look at the engravings and then followed the couple out of the cave.

Once we reached the surface I took a deep breath and was overwhelmed with a sudden desire to call Evie. I wasn't sure why, but from the intensity of the feeling I knew it was important to call. I pulled my cell from my pocket and dialed, hoping the necessary words would form when I needed them. Because right now, I didn't even know what I should say.

"Hello? Christian, is that you?" Evie sounded worried.

"Yes, Evie. It's me. I'm calling to let you know that Justin, Jillian, and I hooked up and are now looking for Rose together." As I listened to Evie exhale a sigh of relief, I felt bad for putting her through all of this. Even though it had been her decisions that led me to leave and search for Rose on my own, I supposed if I was in her position, I would probably be reacting the exact same way. If a new Sire and his hybrid consort both turn dark and then basically disappeared, the rest of my clan's safety would of course become my number one priority. Most of my anger faded away with that realization, but it still hurt that she didn't trust my decisions and abilities as Sire. But then again, I was basically flying blind here, so how could I expect *her* to trust in me when *I* didn't even have a clue as to what I'd be led to do next?

Silence hung on the line as I searched for something to say; thankfully, in the next moment the words filled my mind and spilled from my lips. "Evie, I need you to contact Balam and ask him if he has ever seen any petroglyphs in the caves beneath Chichen Itza."

As the sentence left my mouth my head started to spin. I tried to piece things together; the carvings here in Virginia, Rose, Balam, Chichen Itza. I had no idea how any of it fit, but my gifts were guiding me in a way I'd never experienced. It was almost like I was being led by something other than my claircognizance. I suddenly wondered if Loraine had anything to do with the ideas now floating into my mind.

"All right, Christian. I'll call him as soon as we hang up. Do you want to tell me what this has to do with?" Evie's voice pulled me back to our conversation.

"No, Evie. I'm sorry, but I can't tell you. I just need whatever information Balam will have to share."

I wasn't trying to be an ass, but I simply couldn't discuss what I didn't understand. Maybe once I heard what Balam had to say it would all make sense, but until then, I didn't have a clue.

"I trust you, Christian. I want you to know that. I'll call as soon as I have something." Evie hung up first, because I was still too struck by her words to hang up the phone. *She trusts me.* That was good to hear. Now if I could just start to trust myself again.

CHAPTER SEVENTEEN

Moving Day

(Meredith)

Today was moving day and it was bittersweet. I hated being forced to leave my house, but I was happy to be moving forward with Jeremy and our baby. I only had a few more things to pack and then Jeremy wanted to grab an early dinner while the movers finished the job and transported everything to our new home. They would coordinate with the building's staff to get all of the big pieces into place, allowing me to spend the evening and the following few days unpacking and organizing. I planned to return to work and announce my pregnancy and move by next week, but wanted to get the house set up first. The second I shared my plans with Jeremy, however, everything changed.

"No, I don't think so. I don't want you going back to work at all."

His statement shocked me. "What are you talking about?

Why would I quit my job?"

"Because you're carrying our baby and you need as much rest as possible. I make plenty of money to take care of us and once your house sells, our nest egg will be replenished. There's simply no reason for you to go back to work."

My first instinct was to feel softened by his concern, but as I looked at him and thought about his snap decisions as of late, I started wondering if there was something else going on besides him being an over-protective husband and father. The idea of not working definitely had merit. I could hole up here and not venture out into the world, except to further my cause with the demons. However, I felt the need to put up a little resistance, just to see if I could get any more information as to the true reason behind his feelings.

"But I love my job, you know that."

"Well, I love tequila, but I don't drink it because it's not good for me. This is something that I need you to do for me, Meredith. Just say you'll stay home and take care of our child."

Now I was getting worried. With his reaction to the home

on our search, and now with this over the top concern about the baby, I was starting to wonder if my blood was no longer doing its job. I decided to test my theory and used our mind bond to attempt to change his mind.

As he turned to grab the last box that was sitting on the kitchen counter, he hesitated slightly as I sent the thoughts into his mind, but then, after a slight shake of his head, he lifted the box and walked straight out to the car.

Son of a bitch!

I was on the verge of a serious panic attack. If Jeremy remembered Rose and the fact that I'd killed his wife and Damien...at worst, he'd kill me on the spot—or at least try to— and at best, the wonderful concern he was currently feeling would cease to exist as he ran out my door.

I wiped a single tear from my cheek as he returned from the garage. "Are you ready to go to dinner, honey?" he asked nonchalantly. "I thought we could head to The Melting Pot again."

Yuck. I was so sick of that place. I wasn't sure if it was the pregnancy or not but if I had to dip one more thing into a bowl of melted cheese, I was going to puke. Why couldn't we just go to McCrady's? I was having enough trouble eating anything other than blood, but at least if we went there I could get a good steak tartar.

"Never mind. How about we go to McCrady's instead?"

I spun around, squinting in confusion. If I was just able to change his mind about the restaurant, that meant that the bond was still working. But if that was the case, then why didn't it work when it came to the baby? I tried something else completely random to test my theory.

"That sounds good, how about we take the bus instead of driving?"

"Sure, that sounds great. Let's take the bus."

What the hell is going on? I retracted my last thought from his mind and walked to the car instead. It looked like I was going to have to pay another visit to my grandmother and see if she had any idea as to what was happening, because for the first time in a long time, I didn't have a fucking clue.

CHAPTER EIGHTEEN

Request

(Evie)

I was flooded with relief when I received Christian's call, but when he made his odd request my nerves kicked back up again. As soon as we'd hung up I dialed Balam, just as I'd promised. I still wasn't sure if I should share all the details of our current situation with him or not, but as soon as he answered, I decided to stick only to the information Christian requested.

"Hola, Evie. How are you, my child?"

"I'm good, Sire, thank you for asking. I'm sorry to disturb you, but I'm calling with a special request."

With a light tone to his voice he asked, "And what might that be?"

"I need you to venture into the lower caves below the lair and see if there are any petroglyphs carved into the walls."

"My, my, that is a special and very *specific* request. Is there anything in particular that I'm looking for?"

I knew this was his polite way of digging for more information, so I gave him what I could. "I'm not sure. In an effort to prepare our clan to stand against the demons, I've performed the Passing of Powers ritual with Christian. He is now our new Sire. I've asked that he stay with us until the threat is eliminated, and following his psychic gifts, he's asked that we check for carvings beneath Chichen Itza. That's really all I know."

After a slight pause, Balam replied. "All right. But the caves are extensive and obviously since we can only look at night, it will take some time to cover them all. I'll gather a team and get started right away."

I was so pleased that he didn't question me further because for one, I didn't have any more answers regarding Christian's request, and two, I didn't want to have to lie or hide anything from my Sire about Rose.

"Thank you so much, Balam. I'll be waiting for your call." I hung up before he even had a chance to say goodbye.

I sat in my office, contemplating what it was that Christian could possibly expect Balam to find. It didn't take long before I was rubbing my temples. Pushing away from my desk, I walked out of my office and into the club. I spotted Dax and Terrance looking over the railing from the second floor and made my way through the crowd. I climbed the stairs and eased my way between my consort and his best friend.

My heart swelled as I looked at Terrance. We had almost lost him when Meredith had him under her control. It had been a blessing from the gods that he'd fallen in love with Loraine, as it was *that* connection which had brought him back to us. I felt bad that he would never get the chance to be with the woman he desired and who had ultimately saved his life, but I was so happy we had him back in our clan that I couldn't stop myself from shedding a tear.

"Evie? Are you all right?" Dax reached out and brushed the pad of his thumb over my cheek.

"Yes. I'm fine. Just a bit overwhelmed." I leaned into Dax's embrace while smiling at Terrance. "I'm so thankful that you're back with us, Terrance. I'm sorry I haven't taken the time to say that."

"Thank you, Evie." He clapped Dax on the back. "I'm definitely happy to be able to hang out with this guy for a few more centuries."

Dax and Terrance had been best friends since the day we'd decided to turn him to save his life. When Terrance was infected and facing the potential of the true death, it had really hit Dax hard. This was just another reason I was grateful that Terrance had pulled through. If he would have remained dark, I would have had no choice but to kill him, and I wasn't sure if Dax could continue to love me in the same way, if that had been the case.

Dax must have been scanning my thoughts, because he whispered in my ear. "Nothing could ever change how much I love you."

The emotional rollercoaster I was currently experiencing must have got the better of me, because the overwhelming sense of love and lust I felt for Dax in that moment had me crushing his mouth to mine as I pulled him into the nearest private room. Terrance laughed out loud as he walked away.

After shutting the thick curtains behind us, I led Dax to the velvet couch. I'd always been so involved with being the Sire and making sure everyone else was taken care of, that at times, I forgot to take care of *us*. He always understood and knew it was just part of being the consort of the Sire, but at times like this, when I was emotionally drained, he was the only one who could fill me back up and restore balance to my life.

CHAPTER NINETEEN

Home

(Rose)

After fleeing Mt. Vernon, it only took twenty minutes before I was standing at the entrance to the caves in Hannibal, Missouri. It was nine a.m. and the area was crawling with tourists. I was feeling possessive over the underground lair that awaited me and wanted everyone to leave so I could claim my new home.

Home. The word caused an odd reaction in my brain. First it became a question. Where was home? Then it became a slideshow of memories: a two-story house with a nicely manicured lawn, a night-club with a red sign flashing above its door, and finally an ancient cave where stone and fire surrounded me.

The images were knocked from my mind when someone accidentally bumped into me. The growl that escaped me had the woman backing away with wide eyes. Trying hard to control my bursts of speed I turned and ran toward the tree line that surrounded the area. I had to remain calm or else I'd end up ripping out the throats of everyone around me.

After I was out of range from prying eyes, I leapt into one of the massive oaks. I decided to get some rest while I waited for the tours closed. I leaned back against the rough bark, balancing myself on the thickest branch. The awkward location didn't bother me in the slightest and within minutes I was drifting to sleep.

A roar of threatening menace ripped from my throat. Echoes of terror filtered to my ears as the villagers I now noticed screamed in reply.

I felt myself drifting above the scene. My fangs throbbed at the amount of blood that coated the ground and the strength that flowed through my body had me feeling like a god.

The scene remained the same until a large beast entered the other end of the village. I couldn't hear his words over the buzzing in my head, but I somehow knew he was talking to me. He had long jagged fangs, just like mine, and upon staring a little longer, I could make out large wings that wrapped around his body.

As he moved forward, the tribesmen scattered in all directions like cockroaches scurrying away from the light. The massive winged being stalked toward the center of town, heading straight in my direction.

"Ixtab!"

The roar in my head continued to increase as the creature got closer.

"Ixtab!"

I hovered above the beast and watched as he unfurled his wings. They were leathery—almost skeletal—and stretched at least six feet in each direction. He launched into the air, stretching his hands out to grab me.

It was then that I awoke, screaming and finally free of this nightmare. Birds flew from the tree as the branch shook, setting loose its leaves as if to save them from my wrath. Breathing hard, I quickly scanned the area making sure there wasn't an actual threat. After realizing I was safe, I leapt from my perch. My feet hit the ground, causing a slight tremor. I slowly walked out of the forest and approached the mouth of the cave. A tingling sensation radiated from deep within my belly, spreading up and around to my back.

The temperature dropped as I walked further into the dark. My eyes adjusted instantly and a smile crept across my face. The stone walls were smooth yet jagged at the same time. The ground was compacted from years of tourist activity. There were lights and hand rails that ran throughout the trails, but as I walked deeper into the cave, I knew I'd find areas that were untouched by man. Those were the places calling to me.

When I reached what felt like the center of the tunnel system, I heard a trickle of water as I rounded the corner. After a few hundred feet I came upon a room that had a small pond in its center. Looking to the sky I saw a waterfall that fell from an opening far above straight into the pond below. Besides that hole, the room was a dead-end and therefore had only one main entrance, which meant it was easily defendable. I giggled and jumped into the air, grabbing the edge with both hands and lifted myself out of the opening to scan my surroundings. I found myself deep within the forest, surrounded by ferns and enough trees to blot out the sky. There weren't any trails as far as my eye could see and the hole in the ground was the only additional entrance to the cave system I could find in the area.

I jumped back down and landed with ease. I knew this was going to be the perfect location for me to hole up in. But the question of *why* kept drifting into my mind. I wasn't sure why I felt the need to hide and defend, but as long as this cave served my purpose, I'd remain here while I figured it out.

CHAPTER TWENTY

Mammoth

(Christian)

After I spoke with Evie and gave her my request, Justin, Jillian, and I took off like bullets from a gun. It took a bit longer to reach Kentucky, but we were now standing on the outskirts of Mammoth Cave National Park.

"Come on. Let's get inside and grab a map. We'll split up the sections like we did before," I suggested.

As we raced toward the visitor center, I tried to reach out to Loraine again. She had yet to reappear and my concern was growing. However, before I could sense anything, we were interrupted by a vehicle coming around the side of the nearest building. The headlights hit us before we even had a chance to react.

"Hey, stop right there!" a voice rang out.

Jillian and Justin looked in my direction and within a split second my fangs were buried in the park ranger's neck. I didn't have time to deal with any shit that would slow our progress, but as I erased our presence from his mind, I scanned him to see if there was anything of interest that I should know about within these caves. Surprisingly enough, there was. Apparently, just like the ones in Virginia, there were petroglyphs located in the depths of the caverns, far removed from the normal trails.

As we watched the ranger drive away from inside the main visitor's area, I told Jillian and Justin what I'd seen in his thoughts.

"I want to take that section so I can check out the drawings," I said as I pointed to the map. "Jillian, you take the section with the Frozen Niagara room, and Justin, you head to the Fat Man's Misery." They both nodded silently then kissed each other before breaking apart and heading to their designated areas.

My path led south. I followed curves and corners down and around the cold walls, all while hoping to glimpse something that spoke of Rose's presence. I'd gone about three miles in when I came around a sharp turn and caught myself on the edge of a massive hole. It was impressive and at first glance, could easily be compared to a bottomless pit. Suddenly, the images I glimpsed from the park ranger's mind dimmed in comparison to what I knew was hidden at the bottom of this abyss.

I jumped into the void without thinking twice. I fell for what seemed like twenty seconds with my eyes closed and my hair streaming straight above my head. Suddenly my senses snapped into focus just before I splashed into a sink hole at the bottom of the pit. It was deep, but once I got my bearings I was able to make my way to the water's edge and scrambled out onto what felt like a shell covered floor.

The loose shale that shifted under my feet had me wondering just how deep I was. It was clear that water had constructed this entire wonder; the small river entering one side, spinning in the center, then disappearing back underground, was evidence enough. I was momentarily stunned as I thought about the water and stone locked in a never-ending dance that resulted in this geological anomaly. I closed my eyes and let my senses expand. I listened to the constant ripple of the stream as it ran through the small pool and after a few deep breaths I felt a presence over my left shoulder. I turned back towards the pool to see Loraine hovering over the water, illuminating it and the space around us.

"Loraine. Thank the gods. I've been so worried."

I waited for a response but received none. Instead Loraine's eyes were wide and her mouth open as if caught in a silent scream. The normal light that accompanied her ghostly form began to shine brighter and brighter, basking the entire area in a blinding silver glow.

"Loraine, what's happening? Please, are you all right?"

I shaded my eyes against her ethereal light as I tried to make sense of things. In the thick fog her spirit created, flickering images started to play out like scenes from an old-time movie. Images of blood and violence, rage and murder, complete decimation and utter chaos, all raining down upon hordes of screaming people.

The flashes were so distorted I couldn't piece any of them together, and I certainly didn't understand what they meant or how they related to me or Rose. Once I realized the flashes were all the same, repeating over and over, I decided to focus on Loraine instead of the confusing picture show.

"Loraine. Can you hear me?"

She said nothing.

"If you can't respond, at least give me a physical sign if you can hear my words."

A slight nod to her head was all I got in return. I supposed it should have eased my mind, but in reality, it just upset me even more. I didn't understand why we could no longer communicate. Before I had a chance to form another question, the pictures disappeared and Loraine herself started to flicker in and out. Within moments she was gone again.

"Dammit!"

I paced the cave and ran my fingers through my hair. I had no doubt I had drifted dark again, and at this rate, I'd be surprised if I ever returned to my normal coloring. What was I supposed to do now? This turn of events left me frustrated and unfocused. I had to calm myself if I was to piece together any of the clues—if that's what they were—into information that could help me find Rose.

Sighing deeply, I forced my thoughts back to the reason I was in this hole in the first place...the petroglyphs. I walked around, my eyes slowly readjusting to the dark surroundings. The sink hole was in the middle of the round space, leaving the shale covered ground to circle the pool in a radius of about six feet. The walls surrounding the space were covered in strange vines which seem to burst through the hard surface on a life and death mission in search for the water below. I followed the curve of the room until I reached an area free of tangled roots. This particular expanse of stone was smooth except for the nicks and cracks, indicating the presence of the carvings I was looking for.

I squinted and ran my hands over the entire area. I could make out similar images to the ones in the cave in Virginia: tribesmen farming and herding animals, stars and comets filling their night skies, and adults caring for their children. But it was the warriors posed with spears pointing towards a winged creature that held my full attention.

The carvings were worn but I could clearly see this beast was humanoid except for the massive wings protruding from its back. I followed the image to the right, trying to decipher the ancient story laid out before me. The warriors used spears and arrows to keep the beast at bay, but it wasn't until *another* winged being fought with it in the sky, that the creature actually left the village in peace.

CHAPTER TWENTY-ONE
The Greatest News
(Meredith)

"Grandma, I'm sorry this upsets you, but I hoped you'd be able to help me understand what's really going on."

"I don't know what you want me to say, Meredith. I told you that drinking human blood was going to affect you and the baby. I can only assume the connection you're describing is due to the link the baby has to its father. It's causing a bond between the two that is leaving Jeremy feeling very paternal and protective from the sounds of things. But as to exactly how it works...I have no idea."

Well, shit. While the information was vaguely what I needed, it wasn't exactly the greatest news. It seemed the initial lie I'd told Jeremy about the baby developing a bond to him was essentially coming true. The bond may not be required for its survival, like I'd falsely indicated, but it was certainly one that was making Daddy very "alpha-male."

"Thank you, Grandma. That's all I needed to know. I guess it makes sense that the males of our race would develop a protective nature towards their children. Was Grandpa like that with Mom?"

"No, Meredith. My pregnancy was as normal as any other human's. That's what I'm trying to explain. You, my dear, are experiencing something completely unique, and whether that's good or bad, is something only time will tell."

The tone of her voice and the sadness layering her features portrayed just how disappointed in me she was. My heart began to break. But as she turned to walk away, the fissure stopped— my anger sealing it closed instead.

How dare she be mad at me! I was doing something no other demon had done in centuries. I was ushering our race back into a time of legends and Gods. A time where demons didn't hide their existence but lived openly, practicing the traditions that made us a race to be feared.

As my anger continued to grow, my fists clenched and I felt my eyes flaring red. I moved to confront my grandmother with these very thoughts when it hit me, *This is your grandmother.*

Now I was the one struck by fear. *What is happening to me?* How could I even imagine hurting the woman I'd loved my whole life? Not wanting to do that very thing, I raced from the house, tears filling my eyes. I knew this was the last time I'd be speaking to my grandmother...for her own sake.

People say when you're pregnant your hormones are out of control, but what scared me the most...what if it wasn't my hormones at all? What if it was the fact that I was becoming something I couldn't even control myself?

CHAPTER TWENTY-TWO

Day and Night

(Rose)

It had now been three days since I'd settled into my new *home*. The cave served me well, as my meals—I mean the tourists— walked straight into my lap on a daily basis. I had stopped trying to use my sedative, as I simply couldn't get past the euphoric feeling caused by my kills. Instead, I simply enjoyed the feeling of the blood as it fueled me, boosting my immortal essence. I had also started exploring the surrounding forest both day and night. The tall trees and fern-covered ground were filled with life and death and I felt as if I fit right in. The only thing that continued to disrupt my existence were the reoccurring nightmares I had each time I slept, which lately had become more and more often.

It was as if I was being forced to watch a historical documentary of horrific proportions. One that left me feeling the need to search and destroy everything and everyone in my path. The strong desire to replicate the events had taken on a life of itself. Every time I woke from the terrible dreams I found myself almost flying out of the hole in the cave, searching for the nearest *village* to exact my wrath upon. The feelings were so vivid, so tangible, it took hours after waking to shake them. And at times, my back even ached as if I had been the one flying the night sky, delivering death and destruction.

At the thought, I circled my shoulder blades in an effort to ease the tension building between them, then stretched my arms high into the air. I couldn't understand why I felt so sore and heavy. It was then that I felt something skittering along the ground beside me. When I looked down to my left I noticed something black, moving on the dirt floor. I jumped to the side in an effort to stomp on the creature, but was shocked when it moved in pace with me. I spun in a circle, trying to pinpoint its location.

It matched my movements, spinning and darting with every turn. I felt like I was moving in slow motion, like I was stuck in a dream state where everything remained just out of reach. In an effort to protect my back from the curious critter, I moved to the closest wall. As I flattened myself to the stone surface, the realization of what was happening settled in.

Staring at the black *creature* now lying still upon the floor, I understood it wasn't a creature at all. It was me. The black shredded looking things pooled at my feet were actually dangling from the bottom of my wings.

The last thing I heard before falling unconscious was my own scream, filling the vast cavern.

* * * * *

(Meredith)

After leaving my grandmother's and wallowing in the state of my situation for the next few hours, I'd received a call from Lupé verifying the plans for tonight's meeting at her house. The thought of getting together with the rest of the demons who supported my cause, brightened my mood considerably. Reaffirming that what I was doing was for the good of us all, left me feeling rejuvenated. I had just enough time to return home and change my clothes to go along with the change in my attitude, and to grab a bite to *eat.*

After passing security, I rode the elevator up to our apartment on the twentieth floor. Jeremy was going to be working late, which was customary whenever I had a meeting to attend. He'd always said, *"If you're not going to be there, what's the point of me being home alone?"* It melted my heart. But as I stepped through the door, I heard a rustling coming from the back of the apartment, instantly peaking my curiosity.

"Jeremy, is that you?" I regretted announcing my presence the moment I heard more vigorous shuffling and muffled voices. Quickly dropping my things on the living room floor, I crept down the hall towards my bedroom and suddenly found myself face to face with two vampires.

(Evie)

It was the night after I'd received Christian's call and his odd request. The club was open and the beat of the music was keeping time with my hammering headache. I sat at my desk, staring at the phone, wanting nothing more than to pick up the receiver and dial Christian's number. But, since I hadn't heard back from Balam I truly didn't have anything to report; and if Christian had any good news for us, I'm sure he would have called by now. Forcing myself to move on with our daily activities, I'd sent Dax to ask Renard and Loni to join me in my office.

Walking in hand-in-hand, they both took a seat on the couch and waited for me to begin.

"I've recently secured accommodations for you in Masen. We need the two of you to go back to the location of Meredith's meetings and keep an eye on her. I want to know her every move and exactly how far she's gotten with her plans to feed her people human blood."

"No problem, Evie. We'll leave right away. Where exactly will we be staying?" Loni asked.

"It's a high-rise downtown, here's the address." I handed them the scrap of paper I'd written the information on. "It's not a hotel, but since it's a new structure they have unoccupied apartments that are being rented out for long-term leases. I've secured one on the fifteenth floor for the next two months."

Renard's eyes went wide. "Two months?"

I laughed out loud at his reaction. "I don't expect you to be gone that long, no. But it was the shortest lease I could get. Besides, once all this mess is over, I may just end up keeping it for getaways and to have a backup location in case we ever have to abandon The Rising Pit for any reason."

"Whew." Renard wiped his brow with the back of his hand. "You had me bloody worried there for a moment."

After we settled the remaining details of their stakeout, including a two-week supply of blood bags, I watched as they drove away in Dax's blue SUV.

Returning to the club, Dax guided me through the crowd and back towards my office. "Don't worry, Evie, they'll be fine. And soon, we'll have the upper hand and know just what that bitch is up to."

"I hope so, my love. I hate feeling so useless, and waiting for Balam's response has left me on pins and needles for reasons I don't even understand."

"Well, it's only been one day since you asked Balam to look in the caves. You have to give him some time to complete the task, Evie. Worrying about something that you can't control does no one any good," he said as he placed a kiss on the top of my head. "Patience, my dear, patience."

Listening to Dax rationalize my frustration was rubbing me the wrong way. I knew he meant well, but hearing that I just needed to sit and do nothing, wasn't helping my mood. So, in an effort to rid myself of my headache and my irritation, I left the club in Dax's capable hands and made my way downstairs. Perhaps a nice long bath would help to wash away my stress. Did I really think it would work? *No*...but it was worth a try.

(Loni)

The drive to Masen was quick going as rush hour ended hours ago. In just under two hours we pulled into the underground parking lot of the new building in downtown Masen. It was a pretty impressive high-rise, but to be honest, I was a little concerned. The whole thing seemed to be made of windows and while we didn't burn in the sun, I just wasn't use to being so exposed while I slept.

"Don't fret, love, we're on the fifteenth floor. Any bugger catching a peek up there would have to either be a window washer, or the Amazing Spiderman. Besides that's what they make drapes for." Renard's flippant attitude reminded me of why I loved him so much. He always had a way of putting things into perspective for my overly stimulated brain.

"You're right, of course. Let's get settled in and then head over to Meredith's meeting facility. We still have a good eight hours before sunrise," I suggested.

"Sounds perfect, pet."

We quickly made our way to the fifteenth floor and found our apartment at the end of the hall. The decor was nice, with replicas of fine art hanging on the walls and beautiful vases residing in lighted niches. The kitchen boasted granite counter tops and stainless steel appliances, and the large jacuzzi tub in the master bath had me hoping our stakeout took all two months and then some. The place was gorgeous!

"Wow, swanky," Renard teased.

"It's nice, yeah?"

"Absolutely. But don't get any ideas, poppet, I don't want to be here any longer than necessary. The Rising Pit is our home, and I don't like being away from the family while all this stuff with Christian and Rose is playing out."

He was right, *again*. This wasn't a honeymoon, and it certainly wasn't a replacement home; it was just a means to an end, and that end was getting the low down on Meredith and her demons.

"Let's go," I said, feeling a renewed sense of determination.

Locking the front door and stuffing the key into his pocket, Renard grabbed my hand as we made our way back to the elevator. The doors opened and we stepped in, pushing the button for the ground floor. Unfortunately the elevator was making its assent, so we'd have to wait for its skyward journey to end before we could be on our way. *We should have taken the stairs,* I thought to myself.

We stood in silence, bored as the people moved in and out of the box, entering and exiting onto their chosen levels. It wasn't until we reached the twentieth floor that something caught my attention.

CHAPTER TWENTY-THREE

Trapped

(Christian)

I continued to study the petroglyphs in front of me, following the story they told over and over. It still left me no discernible information relating to Rose, though. However, I did feel trapped by the appearance of Loraine, as if leaving the only place I'd recently seen her would be a mistake.

"Justin, Jillian? Can you hear me?" I shouted.

It took a few minutes before I heard movements from above.

"Christian, where are you?" Justin asked, obviously confused.

"I'm down here. In the sink hole. I've found some more carvings and think that since it's getting close to sunrise we should just stay here tonight."

"Do you want us to come down there with you? Is there a way out?" Jillian called.

"No. Just stay up there. We are far enough off the beaten trail that no one will venture in this far." My claircognizance was kicking in and I knew we'd remain undiscovered while we slept.

"Okay. Sounds good. Neither of us found anything in our areas either, by the way," Justin added.

"I didn't expect you would." I tried not to sound disappointed. It wasn't their fault we were on a wild goose chase.

"Don't worry, Christian. We'll find her soon." Jillian's reassuring words helped a bit, but as I settled down onto the hard ground, the shards of shale poking into my sides, I concentrated on Rose, hoping something would spark. Unfortunately the only sensation I got was that of our bond being stretched far beyond its limits. My body began to shake uncontrollably and it was in that moment, I wondered if I'd actually survive this situation after all.

(Evie)

After soaking my troubles away, I was headache free when Dax joined me once the club had closed. My evening was topped off by a much appreciated massage and the sensual attentions of my beloved mate before we fell comatose for the day.

The following evening, we woke and headed straight to the cooler. Everyone else had already fed and made their way upstairs, so it was just Dax and I in the storage room when my cell phone began to ring.

"Hello."

"Hola, Evangeline. I'm calling with news," stated Balam.

His serious tone put me on edge immediately.

"Just a moment, Balam. Let me get to my office so that I may take notes." I nodded at Dax and flew down the hall and up into my office in a matter of seconds, sealing the bookcase behind me.

"Apologies, Sire. Please continue."

"After searching the past two nights in the caves below, we did discover some ancient drawings in one of the oldest areas."

While I was excited to learn what they found, the hesitation I could sense in his voice had me worried that "excited" wouldn't be the appropriate word for what I was about to hear.

"Evie, I'm not sure if what we found will be of any help to you or your new Sire, but to say that we have discovered some very important information about the demons, is putting it mildly."

The air rushed out of me and I began to rapidly drift as my Sire explained to me the extinction of an entire race.

* * * * *

(Loraine)

The terror was now something I couldn't escape. I was stuck in this hellish ether, forced to witness the end of a civilization over and over again. The images played continuously, until bits and pieces of information started to accompany them. Information I wish I could now forget.

The story had been laid out before me; the demon princess Ixtab, the daughter of Yum Camil, was the Mayan Goddess of Death, Sacrifice, and Suicides. After reveling in her duties as the Death Goddess for centuries, she became bored and jealous of her brother, the bat-God Camazotz. She wanted to have wings and be able to fly like him. So, in an effort to do so, she performed magick chants, offered many sacrifices and finally— in a bizarre ritual—bit Camazotz, becoming the first ever hybrid—his vampire blood mixing with her own.

At first, nothing happened except her desire to drink human blood, but as she continued to perform her godly duties, killing more and more, she eventually developed wings and a thirst for nothing but blood and destruction. This was the hybrid's way of drifting dark.

After leveling villages and slaying her people, Ixtab left Xibalba and began her world-wide killing spree. Yum Camil sent his son, Camazotz, to stop her. He tracked her all over the world, engaging her in fight after fight as he tried to protect the innocent people of the human realm. Eventually, he successfully brought Ixtab back to Xibalba. When she realized she was trapped and could no longer leave their realm, she killed her brother and father in a fit of rage, effectively ending the Mayan race.

Trapped in Xibalba, truly alone—her reign of terror complete—the Goddess of Suicide killed herself, leaving only the human descendants of Camazotz and Yum Camil to carry on in secret, hidden in the folds of time.

CHAPTER TWENTY-FOUR

Power

(Rose)

I opened my eyes and felt death. The presence of it, the weight of it, the power of it. I couldn't believe how good it felt. I thought *the power of it* described it best. It felt like a surge within my soul...one that would only grow stronger.

Sitting up slowly, I took stock of my surroundings. I was still in the cave, laying on the cold ground. But spread out under me, cushioning me from the rough edges of the rock, were my wings.

I *hadn't* dreamt them. They were real.

Standing up, I looked over my shoulder, trying to get a better view. My wings were large, black, and fierce. They looked like dragon hide and had wisps that extended from the ends and edges, making what I was sure would be a frightening sight as I flew through the sky. A sight I had seen often as of late; a sight I had dreamt about for days.

Feeling the rush of anticipation, I extended my arms—not knowing how else to make them move. I laughed as my wings lifted, instantly catching the air currents surrounding me.

With one spin and a slight push off the ground I was hovering in mid-air, as if flying was already second nature. *Wait...what if it was? What if the memories and feelings I've had lately were actually of me doing all those horribly beautiful things?*

Finally awake and aware of what I'd truly become, I shot out of the hole in the top of my cave and went searching for answers. Answers and blood.

* * * * *

(Evie)

"Christian, I need you to call me as soon as you get this message. It's URGENT!! I heard back from Balam, and we need to talk IMMEDIATELY!"

Dammit! I was so pissed right now. This was the fourth time I'd tried to reach Christian and was sent directly to his voicemail.

The idea of Rose drifting dark and turning into that...*thing*, was more than I could process. I needed to tell Christian what he was up against; tell him that his decision had been wrong; tell him that while being the hybrid *would* allow Rose to kill Meredith and her demons, if she'd already transformed, she would most likely not stop there. She would turn on us all, wiping out vampires and demons alike. And worse, unlike Ixtab, Rose had run of the human realm; an entire world to terrorize.

I turned to Dax, who hadn't left my side since finding me hunched over my desk, crying with my cell phone still in my hand. "Do you think I should call William and see if he can reach Jillian or Justin?"

"Yes. That's a great idea. Maybe he'll know why Christian has been unreachable."

I quickly dialed William's number, hoping he'd be able to set my mind at ease.

"William, it's Evangeline. I'm trying to reach Christian and have been unsuccessful. I was wondering if you've heard from Jillian or Justin lately?"

"No, Evie. I'm sorry, I haven't. The last time I spoke with them was right before they left. Justin had relayed that they were taking off to explore some cave systems in the Midwest, but that was a couple of days ago, and I haven't had any reports since."

Caves? Perhaps Christian's gifts have already given him the knowledge of what's happening to Rose. The thought had me panicked and relieved at the same time.

"All right, thank you, William. I'll just keep trying him. Perhaps the caves are what's interfering with my calls. But please, if you hear anything, let me know."

"Of course, Evie. I'll try Justin again right now. Take care."

I hung up the phone and shook my head at Dax. Not that he hadn't heard the entire conversation, but because I just didn't have the words to express how devastated I was.

Rose was a descendant from the demon race, and now—since being turned by Christian, she was only the second hybrid to ever exist, linking her directly to Ixtab. If Rose was reveling in her kills she would have already started to drift dark, so if Christian didn't find her soon, we all might as well line up for the firing squad that was Rose Reynolds.

* * * * *

(Christian)

I woke up in a panic. Most likely because the last thing I'd thought was my imminent ruin. I could feel it. I was running out of time.

I listened closely, waiting to see if Jillian and Justin had risen yet but was only met with silence. Using the nooks and crannies, I scaled the rock, hopping out the top in a matter of seconds.

I looked around and found Justin and Jillian huddled together, still asleep against the far wall of the small stone room.

I paced the tight area, annoyed I had no way of waking them faster. Frustrated, I slid down the wall opposite them and closed my eyes. I figured I should put my time to good use, so after taking a couple deep breaths, I tried to connect with Loraine again.

Ten minutes of meditation and I was no closer to receiving any answers. Thankfully, Jillian and Justin finally began to rise.

"Hey," Justin said upon seeing me.

I nodded my head in his direction as he stretched and stood.

"So what did you find out from the drawings down there?"he asked.

I wasn't sure how to answer. Sure, I could describe the images to him, but what was the point? Besides the connection to the demented picture show my dead mother-in-law had shown me, what good had they served?

"No, not really. Just drawings of the tribesmen's daily lives." I wasn't sure if his hesitation meant he realized I wasn't being completely honest with him, or if he was waiting for me to continue. Unfortunately, I simply didn't have anything else to say. Instead, I removed three blood bags from my backpack and tossed two in his direction. We'd need to feed and move onto our next stop...Missouri.

Jillian woke just as Justin and I began to drain our dinner.

"Morning!" she said with a smile.

She was apparently a "morning person." I probably would have been too if I'd gotten to fall asleep with Rose in my arms. Sighing deeply, I shook my head. None of this was Jillian's fault, and I knew I had to stop feeling sorry for myself, but that would have been a whole lot easier if my gifts had been more active lately. I wasn't used to being this disconnected. First with Loraine, and now feeling as if I was losing touch with all of my abilities. *Maybe I was.*

"So. Any news?" Jillian asked.

"No. But I'm hopeful we'll find something at our next stop." I had to keep up appearances. If they knew how defeated I was feeling, they would report that to William who would in turn tell Evie. Dealing with her reactions was the last thing I needed right now. I hung my head and took a couple deep breaths, but my anger at this entire situation must have caused me to drift again, because when I looked up at Jillian her eyes grew wide. She then quickly made her way to Justin's side, claiming the third blood bag for herself.

I frowned as they both stared at me with open uncertainty. They knew I wouldn't hurt them. *Well, I hope they knew that.* No matter how depressed and upset I got, I wasn't that far gone.

"What's wrong? Why are you both looking at me like that?"

Jillian spoke first after taking a few sips of blood. "Um...well, because Christian...you're glowing."

CHAPTER TWENTY-FIVE

Missed Opportunities

(Loni)

As the elevator door opened onto the twentieth floor, my attention was transfixed on the blur that sped past. A blur that no one, other than Renard and I, would have been able to see.

We looked back and forth at one another as the crowd in front of us shuffled about. Whoever or whatever that was, would have been long gone by now and since we needed to get to Meredith's meeting site, there was simply no time to investigate. But with a nod towards my husband, I verified that I definitely wanted to check it out later.

We completed the torturously slow ride to the ground floor, then finally exited the elevator and then the building. It was faster and way more stealthy to run to our destination, so after a few short minutes on foot, we arrived at the building where we'd previously witnessed Meredith's meetings. Claiming our original stakeout spot, we peered through the window at the east side of the facility. The last time we'd been in this position we'd watched as Meredith spiked the punch with human blood, but tonight, all we saw was a dark, empty room, devoid of any humans or demons.

"Well, shit," I said.

"Guess we should hang around to see if anyone shows up."

"Guess so," I replied.

After hours of waiting in the shadows, and no one making an appearance, Renard stood up and stretched his arms high above his head. "Looks like we'll have to come back tomorrow."

"Why? Let's just run over to her house and see if we can pick up her trail from there," I suggested.

"Evie made it clear we were to stay away from their home. Especially since Jeremy identified me the last time we were there. We can't risk either of them seeing us again or we could blow this whole thing."

"Fine! So what if she isn't here tomorrow either? Are we going to visit every night to make sure we don't miss her?"

"Yes. I suppose we will."

"Dammit!" I really didn't want to spend every waking minute sitting here in the dark, waiting for this bitch to show herself. Bouncing from foot to foot, I decided to run off my frustration by taking a quick lap around the building. I was glad I did.

Smiling as I returned, I waved the piece of paper in my hand at Renard. It was the event schedule I'd grabbed from the glass case mounted next to the front door.

Taking the document from my hand, Renard quickly scanned the planned events for the next month.

"Meredith's name isn't on here anywhere. And even if she was using a fake name, all of these events are either wedding receptions or bar mitzvahs." After shredding the paper Renard shook his head. "It looks like she's moved her meetings, which means we're totally buggered."

Tonight had been nothing but a series of missed opportunities.

After racing back to our apartment, Renard called Evie and explained the brick wall we'd just hit. She wasn't happy, of course, but didn't want us to give up. We were to stay here, and for the next two weeks—which is how long our blood supply would last—go back to the meeting facility and talk to anyone we came across to see if we could piece together where Meredith was now. Evie refused to let us venture to their home; she said she just wouldn't risk us being put on Meredith's radar any more than we had to be. Staking out the meeting facility was the safest bet.

It was three in the morning when Renard hung up the phone. I was frustrated and pretty wound up, so I contemplated how to fill the remainder of our night since sunrise was still a few hours away. *Sex with my husband, or check out the twentieth floor?*

"Babe, do you want to go up to check out that blur we saw earlier? See if we can find out who or what's up there?"

"Not tonight, my sweet. I have other plans for us." He winked.

That answers that. I settled into his arms and let him kiss away the disappointment I knew we were both feeling. We had two weeks to find Meredith and during that time we'd also discover who was occupying the twentieth floor, so tonight...tonight was just about us.

* * * * *

(Meredith)

Staring into the eyes of two vampires in my own home sent me into a full-blown panic. But instead of launching an attack, my fight or flight response had me racing out of the apartment and back down the hallway. I assumed it was due to my *maternal state*. I flew past the elevator, heading immediately for the stairs. I was down twenty flights in a matter of seconds and ran directly to Lupé's house, collapsing at her front door.

"¡Dios mío! What is wrong, child?"

Lupé and her youngest daughter came running out of the house and quickly collected me in their arms. They helped me onto the couch that sat at the end of the porch.

"Thank you." I hating showing any vulnerability in front of people who were supposed to be my lessers, but the surprise of what just happened overshadowed my need for pretenses. "The vampires found me."

Lupé gasped and her daughter, whose name I still couldn't remember, started crossing herself and praying under her breath.

"I'll call Raúl right away. We'll push up the meeting and dose everyone with a larger amount of blood, then we'll *all* escort you back to your apartment. We'll put an end to this." She left my side and headed back inside where I could hear her dialing the phone.

I was so grateful for not only the physical support, but also for the feeling of being truly cared for that her words had created within me. Though Jeremy treated me like a queen and always had loving things to say, in reality it was all a lie. But this—genuine concern from one of my own—was real, and it made me feel good.

I smiled at the young girl and listened to her mother complete what I could only describe as a demon phone chain. Two initial calls went out, then, ten minutes later, people started arriving in droves. I watched in stunned silence as Lupé and her family quickly erected a large tent structure, filling it with tables and chairs in the front yard, while others carried in two humans who were obviously obtained to serve as our sacrifices tonight.

My strength returned and I licked my lips when I saw Juan, another of Damien's cousins, cut a man's throat, draining the life-giving fluid into the large pail that had been placed at his feet. Sacrifices, blood, immortality...all present here in the woods with others of my kind; this was how our ancestors must have lived. The thought had me feeling extremely *primitive* and my craving for blood was quickly reaching an uncontrollable level. All I wanted to do was fly over to the dying man and latch my mouth over his open wound. But, if I wanted to keep the others drinking blood in only small doses, I knew I had to show restraint, however the stress of controlling myself had me shaking in my seat.

"Meredith, are you all right?" Lupé asked upon her return.

I met her gaze with my eyes glowing red. She simply nodded and walked straight over to the table, grabbed a cup, and dipped it into the vat of blood while shooing off everyone who began to question her as she made her way back to my side.

"I think you need this. Though I will have to answer questions from the others as to why they can't drink straight blood too."

After downing the savory contents of the cup, I smiled and said, "Thank you. I'll speak to them."

Lupé began to gather everyone under the large tent, and after Juan and Max, another cousin, disposed of the two bodies, I began my first speech as their true leader.

"Thank you all for coming on such short notice. I'm sure you have heard that the vampires found me, which is the reason for this rushed affair."

I placed a hand over my stomach in an effort to gain sympathy so that my next statement would be taken at face value.

"I asked Lupé to bring me a cup of blood directly from the pail in an effort to replenish and nourish my unborn child. The stress of running across town as we fled for our lives, took a toll on him that required a direct dose of blood to heal. Thankfully the affects are fast acting and the baby and I are now going to be just fine."

The sighs of relief and hushed prayers that floated up from them had me feeling hopeful.

"I want you all to make sure you have an extra cup of *punch* tonight, and then we'll head back into town to investigate together. I'm pretty sure the vampires would not have lingered, but you never know. The more of us there are, the better."

I suddenly stopped and thought about Jeremy. He wouldn't be home until later, seeing as he'd already arranged to work late because of my meeting, but what if he came home early and found his home infested with demons? I couldn't take that chance, so I'd have to call and delay him even further.

"I have to make a phone call, so I'll give you all a chance to drink up, and then we can solidify our plans."

As the crowd began to gather around the punch bowls that Lupé had just finished mixing the blood into, I found a quiet spot in the back corner of her house to make my call. I took a few deep breaths in an effort to pull myself together before dialing.

"Hello, darling. How are things at work?"

"Hi, Mer. I'm fine, just busy. What's up?"

"Well, I was thinking, perhaps I should come meet you for a late rendezvous and we could take in the midnight showing of that new movie you wanted to see?" I tried to keep my voice even and upbeat.

"That sounds great, actually. I have a couple of new clients that just stopped by the office and this will allow me plenty of time take them to dinner and give them my pitch."

Perfect. This gave me plenty of time to investigate, destroy, and recuperate before I had to meet him.

"Where are you meeting your clients for dinner?"

"O'Connors, just down the street."

"Sounds great, darling. I'll meet you there at eleven."

As I returned to the front yard, I noticed everyone was clearly wired. The blood was doing its job. "Everyone gather around," I instructed from the top of the stairs. I paused as they moved closer to my makeshift podium. "I live on the twentieth floor of the new high-rise building downtown. I think it will be wisest for me to enter by myself, since the building has security. Then I'll make my way down to the entrance for deliveries and let you all in. We can take the freight elevator straight up to my floor without being seen. I'll go in first, followed by Raúl, Juan, and Max, then the rest of you follow but remain in the front room unless I call for you."

Everyone nodded their agreement and seemed to be just fine with following my directions. This was exactly how it was supposed to work; the leader leads and the followers follow.

Simple.

As fifteen or so demons loaded into the vehicles, I made sure I was in a car with Raúl, Juan, and Max. I needed to give a little more detail to my main muscle.

"Okay, guys. Once we enter my apartment you'll need to be ready. If the vampires are still there, they will fight tooth and nail to defeat you, but our biggest advantage is that they won't bite us. They know that doing so would give us the upper hand, as our demon blood would infect them."

They nodded their heads and bumped their fists, as I continued. "However, we aren't restricted by their blood. We *can* bite them. So, if you get the chance to sink your teeth into one of them, do it. Draining them will be our best bet of survival since it will weaken them while fueling us."

The back seat was buzzing with excitement. The men were pumped and ready. Now I just hoped that my instructions were accurate. I'd never bitten a vampire before, but didn't think it would be any different than biting a human. Their blood should boost our speed and strength, while making them weaker in the process. It was clearly a win-win.

Once we entered the parking garage, claiming three spaces near the service elevators, I waved at the group of eager demons waiting in the cars as I strolled towards the front entrance. I was a nervous wreck as I walked into the lobby of my building but tried my hardest to appear calm and *normal*. I was worried my anxiety would spike, causing my eyes to flare for everyone to see. That was something I really needed to avoid if I was going to continue my ruse of a happy life with Jeremy and our child. Normalcy was in high demand. I laughed out loud at the irony as I rode the service elevator down to greet my demon army.

CHAPTER TWENTY-SIX

Rage and Rain

(Rose)

The rain pelted my face as I flew through the air but did nothing to cool my rage. While I dipped and dove through the frigid spray, learning the nuances of my newly developed wings, my attention was suddenly drawn to the bodies scattered across the forest floor below. The overgrown ferns and mossy ground-cover hid them from plain sight, but the dried blood still clinging to their bodies drew me in immediately. There were at least twenty bodies strewn across the span of a couple of miles. As I landed near a small group of them, I instantly knew I'd been the cause of their death. The jagged teeth marks left on their throats were a match for my now protruding fangs. Fangs that were longer and rougher than I remembered.

Shaking my head, I tried to recall inflicting this level of mayhem. A vampire only fed once a day, but apparently I'd been killing at least six or more people at a time. Maybe that was why I was sleeping so much. I was ingesting too much blood. Even the thought of the word "blood" caused a smile to spread across my face and a tingling to race through my veins, but it also scared the shit out of me and *that* pissed me off.

I should no longer fear anything, yet here I was, afraid of losing myself to whatever transformation had taken over my mind and body. I hadn't even known I'd been doing any of this; I had to gain control over this situation—over myself, and fast. It wasn't that I minded the killing, as a matter of fact, I was enjoying it immensely, but what I did mind was not understanding or being able to control what was happening to me.

I flew back to my cave, descending through the hole and forced myself to think back to the last thing I remembered about my life before becoming the hybrid.

A man's face filled my mind's eye, a face that I knew should be familiar but wasn't. I tried to muster a memory that would spark some emotion in regards to the image but failed. I simply couldn't feel anything other than the pounding of blood in my head that seemed to be drumming to an ancient tribal beat.

I laid down, closed my eyes, and let the darkness claim me once more.

* * * * *

(Christian)

Glowing?

"What are you talking about?" I asked.

"How else can I say it, Christian? You're fucking glowing!" Jillian responded.

I looked down at myself and found her statement to be true. My entire body was shining like a lighthouse beacon in the dark. The golden light was subtle at first but then grew to an intensity that lit up the entire cavern.

"Holy shit!" Justin declared as he shielded his eyes.

I searched the space for Loraine, hoping she had something to do with this, but when pain started to wrack my body I knew this couldn't be anything good. Whatever was happening to me had nothing to do with Loraine, but with Rose instead.

My gifts finally decided to kick in and it became clear that our consort bond was close to its breaking point. I was losing her. Our ethereal cord was ready to snap and that meant I was going to die in a cave in Kentucky. Worse, it meant that Rose too was on the verge of dying which caused the scream in my throat to burst free.

"Christian, my god, what's wrong, what do we do?" Jillian screamed.

I had no answer for her as I fell to the ground. The painful pull within my chest had me wrapping my arms around my torso just before I passed out.

(Justin)

The second Christian fell unconscious his body stopped glowing. Jillian looked at me, obviously scared and clueless about what we should do. I pulled out my cell phone to dial William for some advice, but quickly found I had no signal this deep within the caves.

"Let's get him back to the surface, so I can call William," I suggested.

Jillian shook her head and stared at me with wide eyes.

I picked up Christian and instructed her to clean up the blood bags and grab our backpack. We wove our way back out of the cave and reached the main opening within minutes. Thankfully, the park had closed over an hour ago, because the second we got service, all of our phones started blowing up.

Jill and I quickly silenced ours. Then I reached for Christian's, pushing the button to mute the incessant notifications. There were at least six messages for Jillian and I apiece, and over fifteen on Christian's phone. It was obvious that whatever was happening was pretty serious.

I didn't want to be interrupted by another security guard so I raced into the nearby woods and placed Christian against the base of a large tree. I immediately dialed William while Jillian paced, her hair and eyes drifting in rapid succession.

"William, it's Justin. What's going on?"

"Oh thank god. Evie has some serious news that she needs to relay to Christian and she hasn't been able to get a hold of him. Are you still together?"

I looked at my unconscious friend and sighed. *This sucks.* "Yes, we are, but unfortunately Evie still isn't going to be able to talk to him."

"Why? What's happened?"

"We don't really know. After we woke this evening he started glowing and then just passed out. He hasn't come to since."

The line was silent except for the sound of William's deep breaths until he asked, "Did you say he was glowing?"

"Yes, do you know what that means?"

"No, but it sounds like some next level shit is going on around here, and I don't want any part of it. I've never seen Evangeline this panicked before, and while I want to help her as much as possible, I refuse to put any of my family in danger. I think you and Jillian should come home."

Fuck! I didn't want to leave Christian and I knew Jillian wouldn't want to stop looking for her best friend, but I had no idea how to convince William that everything would be okay because honestly...I had no idea if it would be or not.

"William, Jillian and I are fine, and leaving Christian alone isn't going to sit well with Evie. With everything else going on, you don't want to start a feud between our clans."

"Christian has been a vampire for even longer than I have; he can take care of himself. Besides, Evie will understand my wanting to protect my clan since that's exactly what she's doing too. No, you and Jillian will come home. Now!"

The last part of his statement was layered with his Sire command. Jillian dropped the backpack next to Christian's still form and within seconds our bodies were being pulled back to

South Carolina of their own accord. I reached for her hand and

watched the tears fall down her cheeks as we were forced to

leave our friend alone in the woods.

CHAPTER TWENTY-SEVEN

Face to Face

(Meredith)

I knew my eyes were glowing red as we crept closer to the door of my apartment. I was so anxious about coming face to face with the vampires again and the ensuing fight, that I could no longer stop my demon traits from presenting themselves. I didn't think the vampires would have stuck around, but if their intent was to end my life, then what better place to lie in wait than my own home. The question that nagged at me, however, was how in the hell had they found me so quickly after our move?

"Okay, this is it. Is everyone ready?"

My crew nodded their responses and in the next second we all rushed through the front door, poised for battle. Immediately, the men followed me into the back rooms of the apartment while the rest of my demon guard staked out the living room as planned. It didn't take long to realize we were alone.

"The place is clear," I called out, putting everyone's mind at ease. Lupé closed the front door and we all gathered to discuss our next step. "Just look for anything out of the ordinary. A piece of paper or even a matchbook lying on the floor could be the clue we need in tracking them down," I ordered.

As everyone began to spread out, I returned to where I'd encountered the vamps in the first place. My bedroom was clean and there was only the slightest hint of ransacking that had been done but nothing seemed to actually be missing. I was getting ready to look in the bathroom when my cell phone started to ring.

"Hello."

"Mer, it's me. I was just wanting to see if you were still planning to meet me at O'Connors? My meeting is done, so I thought I'd call and make sure you were on your way before I left."

I was happy to receive Jeremy's call and know that he was okay, and since this *mission* was obviously a bust, I had nothing to worry about here for the time being. I was suddenly too exhausted to carry through with our plans for tonight.

"Actually, Jeremy, I'm feeling a bit tired and would prefer for you to just come home. I don't think I could sit through an entire movie at this point."

"All right, my dear. That sounds fine by me. I'll be home soon."

I hung up the phone and made my way back to the front room.

"Thank you all for accompanying me here to make sure I was safe. I'm so pleased by how well we came together as a unit to take on this situation. The time has come for us to become the hunters instead of the hunted, and when we do finally face the vampires, I know we'll succeed as long as we stick together."

Everyone smiled and clapped each other on the back.

"Let's plan to meet again at Lupé's next week. We'll discuss the next step in my plan, but for now, I'm going to call it a night. I will take extra security measures, so please don't worry about me."

Lupé stepped forward and gave me a hug. "Be safe and call us if you need anything at all."

"I will, thank you."

I watched as the small group of my demon army made their way back to the service elevator. I knew that with Raúl as my second in command, and everyone on board with the way I was running things, we'd be able to take down the vampires when the time came.

* * * * *

(Christian)

I opened my eyes and darkness surrounded me. I tried to use my psychic gifts to reach out for information, but couldn't. I knew I'd passed out and was now caught in some sort of in-between world. I wondered if this was what Evie had felt like when she'd fallen unconscious after linking to Terrance. I tried to calm myself and blank my mind, just as I'd suggested to her at the time. But unlike Evie's results, clearing my thoughts did nothing to release me from this nightmare. So, instead, I chose to fill my head with images of Rose.

I thought about the first time I'd seen her leaning out of that limousine, her long blonde hair blowing in the breeze; I pictured us sharing our first kiss in the back seat of my car and all the other times we made out during my breaks from work. I let my mind rifle through the next four months of what I thought was utter bliss when Rose had been in hiding with me at The Rising Pit; and finally, I landed on the image of me sinking my fangs into her neck as her eyes glowed red.

After everything we had been through, I was sure that we were going to end up happy for all of eternity; vampires in love, living the dream. But instead, I was trapped in this unconscious hell, literally alone, feeling the cord of our bond preparing to snap and my life about to end.

Just as I was about to take what I was sure to be my last breath, I started feeling a slight tug in my chest. The images started to flicker and suddenly a horrible beast replaced my beautiful Rose.

Its teeth were long and jagged and dripped with blood. It had hideous wings that sprang from its back and carried it up into the night sky as it screamed and screeched like a howling banshee. Its eyes were glowing red and it's long black hair was stringy and flew in every direction. I instantly recognized it from the drawings I'd seen in the cave.

However, it suddenly became clear that the beast I now saw in my mind *wasn't* a delusion or an image of an ancient demon from the past. No...it was the hybrid—it was *Rose*.

I screamed as the anguish of my decision washed over me in a tidal wave of despair. *How could I have been so wrong?* I cried out again as I opened my eyes and found the beast—my Rose— —staring straight at me within this unconscious dreamscape.

She hovered in midair, piercing me with her ungodly gaze.

"Rose? Can you hear me?"

She tilted her head, like a dog does when spoken to.

"Rose. It's me, honey. It's Christian. Can you tell me where you are?"

The odd look on her face caused my heart to break and my despair to grow. She had no idea who I was. Maybe *that's* why our bond was breaking—*not* because she was dying, but because she was lost to me—lost to herself, and no longer the same person; no longer my beloved Rose.

I closed my eyes and let the tears come. I wondered if I would still die if our bond snapped even though she'd remain alive. Or would I simply continue to exist *without* my consort? She was the hybrid and I was just the vampire who'd created her. I had no idea how our differences would affect our bond, but as I contemplated losing my true love forever, suddenly a golden light began to glow behind my eyelids. I opened my eyes, hopeful that Rose was recognizing our connection, but what I saw next had me flying through the black space of this strange realm screaming and crying, desperate to save my own life.

Rose had a hold of the end of our ethereal cord; our *actual* consort bond. It was a glowing thick *rope* that ran between me and her, anchoring into each of our chests right above our hearts, and she was preparing to rip it apart.

CHAPTER TWENTY-EIGHT

Desperation

(Evie)

After receiving a call from William, I experienced a level of desperation I had never known before. He had explained that for some unknown reason, Christian had passed out in the caves he, Jillian, and Justin were exploring in Kentucky. William told me he'd used his Sire command to order Jillian and Justin home, in fear of the unknown danger pursuing Rose would cause if they continued. I understood the desire to protect his vampire children, but the idea of my son being left alone in the woods, unconscious, had me wanting to sink my fangs into William's neck and let the poison of true death flow. I was much older than the young Sire and would prove the winner of any confrontation between us. Dax, of course, talked me out of any vengeance and we were now racing to the spot we'd been told Christian would be.

After three hours of shadow hopping, we found Christian still unconscious at the base of a tree outside of the Mammoth caves just as William had indicated.

"Do you think we should try to scan him?" Dax asked.

"Honestly...I have no idea. I can't deny that I'm nervous to use my scanning ability after what happened to me with Terrance, and with Rose being a demon turned hybrid...truth be told, I'm a little scared to try."

"I don't blame you, sweetheart. Let's just get him home so we can keep him safe and watch over him until, whatever this is, passes. I won't risk you being hurt."

With that settled, Dax gently lifted Christian into his arms, while I gathered the backpack that was lying at his feet. It would be slow going as we headed back to The Rising Pit, but at least I knew everyone in my clan was safe for the moment.

(Loni)

Tonight we took our time as we made our way back over to the meeting facility. There was a wedding reception taking place and after questioning a few of the guests, we quickly deduced that no one present had any connection to the demons we were looking for.

"This is bullshit. I don't care what Evie says, we just need to run over to their house and see what the hell's going on," I snapped.

"As much as I hate disobeying Evie, she didn't use her Sire command to truly keep us at bay, so I think you're right. Because this," he pointed towards the building, "is a complete waste of time."

I was glad my husband saw things my way, but after sprinting across town to Meredith and Jeremy's brownstone, I was now in an even worse mood than before. There was a "For Sale" sign in the front yard and the place was completely empty.

"I don't fucking believe this!" I shouted. Screw being quiet; there was no danger here, since no one was around. "This is ridiculous. First Jeremy moves from Seela and we almost lose him. Then, Meredith moves her meetings and we're left scrambling. And NOW, we try to track them down at their actual home and it's a fucking ghost town. What the hell are we supposed to do?" I blew out a frustrated breath and plopped down on a grassy knoll in the park.

"First things first, Loni. Let's return to the apartment. I'll call Evie again and let her know what we found out. She'll be upset that we went against her wishes, but once she realizes the importance of what we found, she shouldn't be too hard on us."

After wallowing in my pity party for a few more seconds, I jumped up and walked hand in hand with my husband through the streets of Masen. Renard phoned Evie once we returned to our temporary home, and just as expected, she was upset but understood. We were all frustrated by Meredith's disappearing act, but Evie told us to stay put until she had time to do a little more digging on her end.

"So, babe, do you want to go see a movie or something? Or we could check out the twentieth floor like I wanted," I asked.

"I know you want to see what was up there, but it's not like we've been threatened since being here, and honestly, I'm just not up for any more drama tonight. Can we just go see a movie and enjoy ourselves until Evie has some news for us?"

The moment he pulled me close and placed a kiss on my lips, I forgot all about the blur we'd seen on our first night. "You got it sugar, that sounds great."

I changed out of my *secret mission* clothes, sliding into my skinny jeans, converse sneaker wedges, and a black tank-top that was a little dressier than my previous attire. There was no need to rush at this point, it was barely after eight p.m. and we'd already eaten from the blood bags before we'd left the apartment initially. So, with no pressing business we headed out to enjoy the rest of our evening.

CHAPTER TWENTY-NINE

On Edge

(Meredith)

After spending the day rearranging furniture and finally unpacking the last few boxes from our move, I'd showered and was ready to spend the evening with my wonderful fiancé. I had already slipped Jeremy some of my blood in his morning coffee as usual, so I hoped that I could make plans for tonight without any hindrance from our mind bond going *wonky* again.

"Darling, what would you say if we headed out for a drink and the movie we missed last night?"

"Sounds perfect. Let me just grab my jacket."

Good. I already knew that a glass or two of sparkling cider wasn't going to quench my thirst, so I'd just have to excuse myself during the movie to "use the restroom" and find myself someone who would.

As we locked up our apartment and walked toward the elevator, Jeremy's cell phone started to buzz. After a quick look at the text he nodded his head and smiled.

"What's that about, dear?"

"The clients I met last night liked my proposal and want to expand the campaign a bit. They asked if I could meet them at O'Connors again to get the rest of their ideas down before they leave town tomorrow morning. Do you mind if I take care of a little business tonight before our movie?"

"Not at all."

I loved seeing my future husband be so successful in his work, but it was the fact that this gave me the perfect opportunity to excuse myself from their meeting and find someone to drain, that had me agreeing to the interruption of our date night without any hesitation.

I couldn't deny that my thirst was becoming a problem. One that had me on edge. I kept thinking back to my grandmother's words, *"...I can tell that you are changing, and I'm afraid that what you've started will not be good for our race."* I didn't see how becoming an immortal could be a bad thing, but the closer I got to immortality, the more out of control I felt.

I continued to contemplate the best way to maintain the course I'd set for myself and my race, without losing myself in the process. But every time I'd start to think about cutting back on the amount of blood I was consuming, the physical reaction I experienced was a big indicator it simply wasn't an option.

After parking the car, Jeremy and I walked down the street and around the corner to the restaurant. The warm breeze blowing the scents of the city in my direction had me craving the taste of blood even more so than at Lupé's the previous night. While we waited in the lobby of O'Connors, I scanned the crowd to see whose neck I would be feeding from tonight. The hostess might have moved to the top of my list if she hadn't rushed Jeremy and me to a table almost immediately.

"Would you like to order a drink while we wait?" Jeremy asked as he pulled out my chair.

"Actually, if you could order me a glass of sparkling cider and have it placed at the bar, I would appreciate it. I'm going to excuse myself to the restroom and allow you to conduct your meeting in peace." I leaned down and kissed his cheek. "Just come find me when you're done."

The quick wink he gave me and the sensuous smile that layered his handsome features had me excited for the rest of our evening.

I made my way to the restroom, slipped on my gloves, and claimed the largest stall at the end of the row. I hid inside with the door unlocked, anxiously awaiting my next meal. Luckily it didn't take long until a middle-aged woman strolled into my grasp. I snapped her neck before she even realized I was there. The taste of her blood was so appealing, I knew I'd never be able to go back to not drinking straight from the vein. *God, I sound just like a fucking vampire.*

After I swallowed the last drop, I laid her body on the tiled floor of the restroom, taking a moment to smear some of her blood on the toilet. I hoped it simply looked like she'd fallen and broke her neck.

I removed my gloves and placed them in my purse. Then, making certain I was alone, I washed my hands and exited the restroom. It had only taken two minutes to drain my victim and as I took a seat at the bar, my glass of cider was placed in front of me. I took a sip and closed my eyes as the smooth flavor blended with the blood still coating my throat. I had never done drugs as a kid, but I was pretty sure this was what being *high* felt like.

I continued to sip my drink while glancing at the menu the bartender had slid in my direction. An amused giggle boiled to the surface, which I quickly coughed away. I found the idea of eating solid food hilarious at this point, but my humor faded when I thought about how difficult this was going to become. How would I explain to my fiancé that I no longer wanted to eat? I supposed I could always order a plate and fake my way through a meal like a toddler trying to push his peas around the dish, but sooner or later, he was going to notice that I wasn't consuming regular nourishment.

Relishing the last drop of my blood-tinged cider, I set the empty glass back onto the bar. I glanced at my watch then turned to look over my shoulder towards Jeremy's table. My smile fell and my eyes flared red when I focused on his clients.

They were the same two vampires who had invaded our apartment.

$$* * * * *$$

(Rose)

"Rose? Can you hear me?"

A strange voice pierced the dark. I turned in its direction and tilted my head. There was a figure in the distance.

"Rose. It's me, honey. It's Christian. Can you tell me where you are?"

I frowned as I tried to place this person; place his voice. I knew he should be familiar to me, but I couldn't find the connection. He started crying and a flicker inside my chest flared. I looked down and saw a strange golden cord attached to my heart. It spanned the distance between us and connected me to this man...this *stranger.*

My anger boiled to the surface. I had no control over what was happening to me and it now looked like someone else was trying to control me as well. *No!* I reached down and grasped the glowing rope and pulled. The man flew through the air screaming, but then fell to the ground the instant the cord snapped in two.

CHAPTER THIRTY

My Purpose

(Loraine)

I materialized on a strange realm. A realm I didn't recognize. But it only took seconds to understand my purpose here.

Christian was lying on the ground and Rose was hovering in midair, opposite him. My beautiful daughter was now a frightening beast and her hands were still wrapped around her end of their ethereal cord. I looked down and saw their bond snapped in two, lying at my feet. I quickly picked up both ends and felt the surge of energy flow through me. Christian floated into the air, dangling from his end, and Rose was held in place by hers.

I wouldn't let go and if this was the end for me, I was okay with that. I closed my eyes and held on tight. I was now the astral bridge between my daughter and her consort. Christian may be the one person who could save my daughter, but it was clear that I had to save their bond in order for him to even have a chance.

We hovered in this empty space, frozen in stasis, until a jostling on Christian's end grabbed my attention. I opened my eyes and could thankfully now see past this dreamscape as if I was looking through a cloud. I watched as Evie showered Christian with concern and care, while Dax lifted him into his arms. As they began to walk away, I felt a pull as if we were all being forced to float along behind them. I glanced in Rose's direction and noticed the movement had caused her to stir as well.

* * * * *

(Rose)

I was locked into a paralyzed state the moment the white woman held the glowing cord in her hands. The energy that linked me to that man surged from him, through her, and straight into me. An odd sensation flowed from the woman; a strange connection that washed over me; a connection that was penetrating deeper into my being with every passing second. I couldn't understand it and that made me want to rip these people to shreds.

I was stuck on this astral plane but could also feel the connection to my true body. I realized I was flying through space; flying somewhere this woman was leading me. I assumed this was how I had flown and killed without realizing it before; my mind was stuck in this dream-state while my physical body was fully functioning in the real world.

With my mind a flurry of dazed confusion, I shook my head and confirmed that once we got to wherever I was being forced to go—and my mind and body were joined again—I was going to destroy everyone in my path. The images of death and destruction I'd dreamt about were now the same picture I was planning to paint.

* * * * *

(Evie)

I continued to cry as Dax placed Christian on his bed. He hadn't woken once during our journey home, and I was at a complete loss as to what we should do next. I debated calling Balam again, but thought it was highly unlikely he'd have any advice regarding our current situation. When he'd explained the story of Ixtab to me, his final words had been, *"Good luck, my child. I fear you are facing a very difficult time."* What an understatement.

Dax wrapped his arms around me and asked, "What should we do, Evie? I feel so useless. Are you sure you don't want me to try to scan his thoughts? Even if I'm knocked unconscious, you can always link to me and guide me back the same way I did for you."

I spun around in his arms and looked up at him through my tear-filled eyes. "No, Dax. I won't risk it. We have no idea what's causing Christian's condition, so that solution may not even work. No. We just have to wait until he comes out of it on his own."

I turned back towards Christian and simply stared at my first vampire son, hoping for nothing less than a miracle. We stood over him for what seemed like only minutes when a scream pierced the air. In reality, an hour had actually passed while we stood vigilant and it was now just past three a.m. as Dax and I raced from Christian's room and flew up the stair into The Rising Pit. Luckily it was Monday and the club was closed, so there were no patrons to slow us down.

"What's happened?" I demanded.

"There's something scary as all shit out there. It's got big wings and is hovering in mid-air, just out front of the club," Tori replied.

I walked to the entrance, already dreading what I was about to see, and peered out the small round window in the front door. The image that greeted me had me sinking to the floor and shaking my head in denial.

Dax flew to my side and threw the lock. "My god, Evie, what is it?"

"I know what's happening to Christian. He's dying, and we are *all* next."

CHAPTER THIRTY-ONE

Live or Die

(Meredith)

Staring down these vampires in the middle of a restaurant was the worst case scenario. Especially since this time my fight or flight response was definitely leaning towards the *fight* side of things. I was ready to tear this place apart to get those assholes away from Jeremy. Luckily they saw me before he did and immediately brought their meeting to an end. One shook Jeremy's hand, while the other gave him a pat on the back, then shot me a smug smile. *Oh, these guys are going to pay!*

As I watched them slink out the exit, I realized that I didn't recognize either of them as being part of Evie's clan, which meant that someone else was onto me. *Shit!*

I thought of chasing after them and getting some answers, but as I watched Jeremy stroll through the crowd to reach me, I knew this fight would have to wait. I wouldn't risk destroying the life I was building with him by jumping the gun with one rash move. I truly loved this man and would live and die for him, therefore I had to plan my attack with the utmost care. But now that I'd been located yet again, I knew I couldn't avoid it any longer. I'd have to call Raúl and have him boost the rest of the army's intake of straight blood. I needed them stronger and faster and I needed it now.

"Meredith, are you all right?" Jeremy's question snapped me out of my internal strategizing.

"Yes, I'm fine. How did your meeting go?" It was going to be imperative to get any information Jeremy had on these two vampires, and then...let the hunt begin.

* * * * *

(Christian)

The surprise I felt when I came to left me shocked and confused. I was still stuck in whatever unconscious state I'd encountered Rose in, but was now being held in place as Loraine hovered between the two of us, holding our broken ethereal cord in each of her hands.

Rose was hovering in midair on the opposite end of the glowing rope. Realizing there was no escape from the strange embrace we were all locked in, I took this time to really look at her; to try to find some semblance of the woman I loved hiding beneath this beast. Her hair was dark as coal and she had long, jagged fangs. Her wings were large and rough, with what looked like a stringy gray and black film dangling from the ends. She looked gaunt and bone thin, like she was wasting away, or possibly becoming something more animal than human.

I jerked my head away and closed my eyes at the thought. I let the wave of despair wash over me and sunk into the fact that I had been completely wrong. I never should have changed her. So much for trusting my gifts. *Ha! My gifts? What a joke.*

It was then a surge within my chest caused me to open my eyes.

Loraine tightly held our severed cord while staring directly at me. Suddenly it was as if I could see through her eyes, and what I saw brought sweet relief to my previous hopelessness.

Dax and Evie were carrying me through the woods and thanks to my claircognizance flaring to life, I instantly knew we were headed home. I immediately regretted mocking my gifts as I looked across the misty space and watched as Rose closed her eyes and floated along with us.

It was in that instant I knew we still had a chance to survive this. All of us. I sank into my meditative state and threw my energy and thoughts directly through the cord at Loraine.

"Loraine. Can you hear me?"

"Yes! Oh thank goodness, Christian. Are you all right?"

"I am now. Everything is going to be just fine. But I do need your help."

"Of course. I'll do anything. Just tell me what you need."

"All right. I need you to open yourself up to me. Try to see my energy as it flows from me, through you, and into Rose. Can you do that?"

"Yes. I think so. When I grabbed the broken rope between the two of you, a surge of energy shot through me and has continued to flow at a steady pace ever since."

"Good. That's exactly what we need. I'm going to try to fuse my thoughts to the energy that is flowing between us, and hopefully this will allow me to reach Rose's mind."

"Okay, Christian. I'm ready."

Loraine closed her eyes and took a deep breath. Her ghostly form started to glow a little brighter and I knew this was going to work.

I centered myself and brought the image of when I held Rose in my arms as I changed her to the forefront of my mind. I layered it with the words of the consort ceremony and in a surge of energy, cast my thoughts outward, through Loraine, and directly into Rose's heart.

CHAPTER THIRTY-TWO

Battle Plans

(Meredith)

As the lights dimmed in the theatre, the idea of actually sitting through a movie right now struck me as utterly ridiculous. I was contemplating using my mind bond to force Jeremy to scrub the rest of our evening and call his "clients" back to meet him again. Unfortunately, I knew nothing like that would work. I was sure Jeremy would have a message saying they decided to go with another firm for their marketing when he returned to work on Monday. Now that they'd located me, they wouldn't need to keep up their fake roles any longer.

"I'm excited to see this movie, sweetheart. Thanks for waiting for me at the restaurant," Jeremy said.

"It's no problem, darling. I'm happy your new clients love the plan you've put together for them. Where are they from, anyway?"

"They said they were leaving in the morning to head back home, but they never actually mentioned were *home* was."

Dammit. I needed information, but they'd been careful to not give Jeremy any that I could use. As much as I wanted to buck and rage at that fact, there was no point in worrying about it now. So instead of contemplating about the looming fight, I decided to curl up next to Jeremy and enjoy our time together, because tomorrow I'd be immersed in blood and battle plans.

* * * * *

(Loni)

Renard and I arrived at the theatre, grabbed some candy, and claimed our seats in the highest row possible.

"When was the last time we actually went to see a film?" Renard asked.

"I don't know, which means it's been too long." I leaned in and kissed him long and slow. I loved making out at the movies. It brought back memories of when we'd first met at

Grauman's Chinese Theatre almost eighty-six years ago.

Breaking our kiss, Renard laughed. "You don't want to miss the beginning, do you? It's starting."

After placing one last peck on his lips I turned my attention to the screen and spent the next two hours completely engrossed.

The movie was better than I expected and had even brought an unexpected tear to my eye a couple of times.

"Are you ready to head back to the apartment, or would you like to take another stroll through town before morning?" Renard asked as we made our way to the exit.

I was just about to voice my answer when I stopped dead in my tracks.

I found myself staring directly at Meredith and Jeremy. They were in the crowd just ahead of us, making their way to the side door that led directly to the parking lot.

Holy shit!!

"Holy shit! Renard, look. That's Meredith and Jeremy. They're right there in front of us!"

"Calm down, Loni. Don't give us away. Let's tail them and then we'll finally have some positive news to report to Evie."

We hung back and melded into the shadows that the dark theatre provided. With each step the couple took towards the exit, we mirrored them from our veiled position. It didn't take long until we all emerged from the theatre, at which time we raced around the corner, ensconcing ourselves in the dark alley that ran between the building and the parking lot.

"Do you still have them?" I asked.

"Don't fret, love. You know how good I am at my job." Renard winked. "We won't lose them."

We watched as Jeremy and Meredith walked down the street hand in hand, until they rounded the corner and came to the parking garage of a tall office building. The deep expanse of shadows the garage provided allowed us to get even closer. We continued to watch as the couple entered their car and pulled out of the structure and onto the street.

We tailed them for a few blocks and were stunned when we all arrived back at *our* apartment building.

"What the fuck? How is this even possible?" I asked Renard.

"Guess we know who the blur on the twentieth floor was now, don't we?"

I squinted my eyes and scrunched my nose at him. I'd *told* him we should have checked that out before. I couldn't believe the demon bitch we'd been looking for this whole time was literally living right above us. I was in shock. We hung back until the elevator closed and then watched as the numbers ascended, finally confirming our assumption when they halted at "20."

We immediately raced up the stairs and practically flew into our apartment. Renard had his cell phone open before I'd even shut the door.

"Evie. We have news. Wait...what? Now?"

I didn't like the panic I heard in Renard's voice.

"All right. We'll be right there," he stated.

"Why didn't you tell her about Meredith? What's going on?"

"We have to leave...NOW!"

CHAPTER THIRTY-THREE

Piece of Cake

(Meredith)

After returning to the apartment I was resolved to the fact that my attack on the vampires needed to happen sooner rather than later. I refused to continue being stalked, which was exactly how I felt, now that another set of vampires had found me. *No.* It was time to take our stand.

I used my mind bond to send Jeremy straight to bed, then made my way to Lupé's with multiple donors in tow.

"Meredith, you need to control yourself. There are too many dead bodies piling up," she declared.

I looked across the lawn and saw my entire demon army drinking human blood straight from the source; I could only smile at my guaranteed victory. "I'm sorry you disagree with my methods, Lupé, but you are the one who suggested we bring everyone in to help get revenge for Damien's death, and now that I want to actually attack the vampires responsible, you're getting cold feet?"

I didn't wait for her response before placing my mouth back over the open wound of the woman currently dangling from my grasp.

"You have become lost in the blood, child. You are not thinking clearly. You can't just go to The Rising Pit and declare war. You have no idea what will happen if you do."

"That's where you're wrong. I know exactly what will happen. We'll engage them in a fight and once they ingest our blood, we'll be able to forge a mind bond with them. Then I'll force their Sire to eliminate her entire clan. Piece of cake."

"Piece of cake? Meredith, you know that won't work. They won't bite any of you. They are *very* aware of the poison our blood holds for them. No. This plan is bound to fail and I won't be a part of it."

I was sick to death of having to explain myself. I let my eyes flare and dropped the now dead woman to the ground. Taking a step towards Lupé, I made sure to keep my voice low and stern when I gave her my response.

"Who said anything about them needing to bite us?"

* * * * *

(Rose)

I could feel that my physical body had come to a stop. I was hovering in midair in both the real world and this dream-like state.

I watched as the man sat on the ground, crossed his legs, and closed his eyes, while the white woman remained immobile between the two of us. She, too, had closed her eyes and was now emitting a light glow.

Uninterested in what either of them were doing, I closed my eyes as well. However, the moment I did, I was hit with a massive surge of energy.

I shuddered as if I'd been struck by a physical blow but once I recovered, images started to invade my mind, accompanied by words that caused my heart to race.

My thoughts grew calm as I heard his voice inside my

head. *"Your life to me, my life to you, through this bond our love is true. Whatever shall come, we share in whole. Life to death, eternity our goal."*

My body shook once again. The phrase kept repeating as the images spun as if on a film reel. Moments of me—the me I used to be—and this man locked in a passionate embrace; the two of us kissing, naked in bed; myself working at the club, the club I now recognized as The Rising Pit. All these memories threatened to overwhelm me if not for the mantra repeating in my head.

"Your life to me, my life to you, through this bond our love is true. Whatever shall come, we share in whole. Life to death, eternity our goal."

Finally recognizing the man, I called out, "Christian!" Staring at me from across this open expanse was Christian; my lover, my Sire, my *life*. He had turned me into the hybrid in hopes of stopping Meredith, the demon bitch who was controlling my dad. Everything rushed back to me in a split second. More and more energy surged between the two of us as the cord that held our bond in place started glowing ever brighter as pulsing, bright golden strips of light raced from him to me.

The white woman's form grew brighter and brighter, until it shown like the midday sun. As a massive burst radiated from her she fell to the ground and our cord was fused together once more.

Christian raced to the woman...*Oh my god*...to my mother!

"MOM!!!"

* * * * *

(Christian)

The moment Loraine opened herself up to my energy I knew I'd be able to save Rose. I felt our connection strengthen with each passing moment.

I sent random images of us together, along with the words from our consort ceremony, on a repeating cycle into her mind. Images and words that I hoped would bring her back to me.

Once I felt my energy fuse with hers I opened my eyes. I wanted to cry at the scene before me. Bright golden streams of light were shooting down our ethereal cord, brightening Loraine as they passed through her on their journey towards Rose. *My Rose.*

She was currently looking right at me through silvery-blue eyes. Her hair was starting to lighten but quickly drifted past her usual blond, settling instead on pure white. Her wings, too, were transforming, losing their hideousness and changing into something more dainty and angelic, though they remained black as night. She was a sight to behold.

I shielded my eyes as the light Loraine was emitting reached its pinnacle, bursting from her and knocking her to the ground as our ethereal cord was fused back together.

I raced to her side as Rose cried out, "MOM!!"

CHAPTER THIRTY-FOUR

Horrible Sadness

(Rose)

Everything was happening so fast. Memories of my life flooded my mind and now I was staring at the ghostly form of my dead mother, lying on the ground before me.

"Christian, how is she here? What's happening?"

Christian reached up and smoothed my hair with his hand. The emotion in his eyes had me melting but both of our focus was brought back to my mother as he began to explain.

"Rose, I think your mother just saved us. She was the conduit that kept our bond whole until I had a chance to bring you back from drifting dark."

I looked at my mom and was flooded with such gratitude but also a horrible sadness. I wanted to scoop her into my arms, but knew I couldn't as my hands would mist right through her.

"Is she really gone this time?" I asked.

"Yes, Rose. I think she is."

* * * * *

(Christian)

I held Rose in my arms on this astral plane as she mourned her mother's death for a second time. When Loraine's body finally shimmered and dissolved into the ether like a million tiny fireflies, I worried that Rose wouldn't be able to handle the overwhelming grief of such a tragic event. But as I held her tight, and thought about the transformation she'd just gone through, I knew that the love we felt for one another was so strong that we'd never have to worry about losing each other again.

"Rose. I think when you're ready, if we just concentrate on our conscious selves, we should be able to break free from this place and awake back in our actual bodies."

"Okay, Christian. I think I'm ready," she replied.

We both stood and held hands, closed our eyes, and allowed our thoughts to meld. I tried scanning her, and for the first time ever, I could actually read her thoughts. I could see that her physical form was hovering just outside The Rising Pit.

My eyes flew open and I found myself lying on my bed. I raced from my room and up the stairs and straight out to my beautiful wife who was waiting for me.

The moment I stepped in her direction, her eyes too snapped open and she slowly drifted to the ground. Evie and the rest of the clan gathered behind me. Apparently, they too had witnessed Rose's transformation from inside the club.

"Christian? Are you all right?" Evie asked in a low whisper.

"I'm fine. We're *both* fine." I nodded at Rose.

A smile crept across her face and within seconds she was nestled in my arms again. I hugged her fiercely, taking care not to crush her soft wings.

"Christian. I love you so much!"

"I love you too, Rose. I'm so sorry about your mother. I wish there had been time for you to actually speak with her."

She didn't say another word but simply buried her head in my chest and let her soft tears continue to fall.

* * * * *

(Meredith)

The moment I'd grabbed Max and forced my bleeding arm into his mouth, everyone started screaming at me.

"Shut up! You will *not* question me! I am your leader and I know what I'm doing will work."

I threw Max to the ground and tested the mind bond I'd just forged with him by instructing him to pick up the knife that rested on the decrepit picnic table nearby.

I was thrilled when he did exactly as I'd instructed.

A hush came over the crowd and everyone stared at me with a mix of fear and respect. I knew this was the demon equivalent of being a vampire's Sire. Once my demons ingested *my* blood, they'd do exactly as I commanded. The similarities between our races where shockingly obvious the closer I looked.

"I know you won't agree, but by Max making this sacrifice, we will be able to defeat the vampires in one swift move. All we need to do is get his blood into their Sire and I'll be able to control them all."

The shocked expressions and wide-eyed stares that I received in return pissed me off. How dare they not fall in line with my plans? What about this didn't they understand? The loss of one would guarantee our victory. *What the fuck is their problem?*

"Meredith. Max isn't just a soldier in your army, he's my nephew and a part of this family. How can you even consider doing this?" Lupé questioned.

"Just like this."

I sent the command for Max to cut his own throat and rushed to his side to place a collection bucket beneath him as he fell to the ground.

Silence hung in the air for no more than two heartbeats, then screams turned to howls and in the next second I was being rushed by the entire crowd.

CHAPTER THIRTY-FIVE

Fierce

(Christian)

Once everyone recovered from the shock of the scene in front of them, we all made our way back into the club.

"So, you're saying that Rose is cured from the hybrid's version of drifting dark?" Dominique's question was layered with skepticism.

"Yes, Dom. That's what I'm saying. The spark of love that I was able to ignite within Rose is what brought her back to us. Just like what happened to Terrance because of Loraine."

Rose remained quiet as everyone stared at her. I hated that she was so uncomfortable, but with everything that had transpired, her altered appearance was a lot for everyone to take in. She was beautiful yet fierce, and the lust I felt for her in this moment was beyond compare. I could no longer sit here and answer questions from the clan, I had to be with my consort...to be with *my wife,* before one more second passed.

"I'm sorry, but if you'll all excuse us, we'd like to be alone. Rose needs some time to adjust and process everything that's happened as well."

Rose must have been thinking the same thing because she smiled and reached for my hand, allowing me to lead her to the spiral staircase under the stage that descended into the pit.

"Thank you." Her voice was tentative.

"You're welcome." I squeezed her hand and hoped the look on my face portrayed the immeasurable amount of love I felt for her.

Once we reached our room, I only turned on the light in the corner. The moons and stars that still hung from the ceiling started to sparkle and shine. "Is this going to be okay?"

I wasn't sure if it was too fresh a reminder of her mother or if it would act as a comforting gesture like I hoped.

She didn't answer, but instead guided me to our bed and pulled me down beside her. We laid in silence and watched the crystals twinkle and spin. Minutes passed before she spoke.

"Christian, I did some really bad things while we were apart."

"It's okay, Rose. I forgive you. I forgive you for everything. For keeping secrets, for lying to me, for leaving me the moment you awoke as a vampire. I *completely* forgive you. While your mother was here she was able to fill me in on everything. I know you were only trying to protect me."

I felt her release a breath and prayed my words brought her some measure of comfort. I hated the idea that she felt guilty for her actions, when I was the one who'd not been there for her as her Sire like I should have been.

I was just about to express my own apology when suddenly she crushed her lips to mine.

(Rose)

I wound my hands through Christian's hair as I climbed on top of him. The feel of his strong arms around me as his hands explored my curves had me writhing against him. We kissed and fondled each other with an intensity that rivaled the great love stories throughout history, and while I knew the timing was probably wrong, I simply couldn't wait.

Lifting his shirt above his head, I took a moment to revel in the sight of his chiseled chest. His thick muscles and smooth skin created the perfect canvas for my mouth. Christian's breath grew heavy as I licked and nipped my way across his pecs.

In a rush of speed, Christian ripped my blouse open, taking care to not snag my wings. His tongue went straight to work. With my legs wrapped around him and his mouth at my breast, I closed my eyes and let myself fall into his expert hands.

We made love with a passion that transcended time as our minds and hearts truly connected. Our consort bond flared to life and set the room alight. Maybe we glowed because I was the hybrid. But to be honest, *I* liked to think it was because our love burned hotter than anything either of us had ever encountered before.

* * * * *

(Meredith)

It took some doing, but I'd finally fought off most of the idiot demons who decided to challenge me. My numbers had dwindled because of this little hiccup, but I still had plenty of demons who were now truly scared of me and wouldn't even think of going against me again. With that settled, we'd be able to move forward with my plans to attack the vampires...tonight.

"We simply need to fill these syringes with Max's blood and whoever gets close enough to Evangeline just has to inject her. Once that's done, I'll be able to use my mind bond to control her since the blood is so fresh."

They all nodded their heads. After filling twenty shots, we all loaded into Raúl's SUV and took off for Seela. I was so pumped to put an end to these pests tonight that I hadn't even bothered to wash off the blood that saturated my clothes and skin.

We exited the freeway a couple of miles before the turnoff to the club, using the back roads to get close, then ditched the SUV.

"It's imperative that they don't hear or see us until I give the signal to attack," I explained.

My demons once again nodded their understanding.

We quickly made our way through the forest to the club. I watched from the shadows as two vampires exited a blue SUV and made their way towards the front door. The same SUV I'd seen outside my old house just last week.

I burst from the bushes and flew to within inches of the couple. They spun around and assumed a fighting stance, then called to their Sire—exactly as I wanted them to do. Their eyes grew wide as my army joined me on the parking lot of The Rising Pit.

In seconds Evangeline and the rest of her clan emerged from the club and faced off with us.

"How dare you come here!" Evangeline bellowed.

I laughed at her stupidity. "Did you think I wouldn't come for you after you tracked me down and threatened my life with Jeremy?"

"We didn't threaten anything. You are the one who started this war when you infected Terrance and killed Rose's mother."

"Speaking of Rose...where is my precious, soon-to-be step-demon?"

A vicious roar pierced the air, causing my entire army to cover their ears. I looked up to a see a winged creature with sharp fangs hovering directly above us. A few of my demons started to make a run for it and the rest of us watched as it snatched them up and ripped them limb from limb in one swift move. There was no escaping whatever this was...

"Oh my god...*Jeremy?*"

CHAPTER THIRTY-SIX

Protect My Own

(William)

I waited inside the apartment I'd secured on the eighteenth floor for my vampire strike team to return with the prize I'd sent them to claim. They walked through the door with Jeremy in tow just after three a.m. All I had to do now was change him into a hybrid, just as Christian had done to Rose, and then I too would be able to protect my clan in this upcoming battle against Meredith and her demons.

I'd been so grateful when Evangeline had informed me of the situation and explained her plans for securing a place in Masen to gather intel from. It was then and there I decided I'd do the exact same thing, only for a different reason. I'd sent Bryce and Nicholas with a picture of Jeremy, one that I'd gathered from Jillian's scrapbook of her times spent with Rose and her family.

I'd been thrilled to receive the report they had actually run across him on their second night as they rode the elevator to the apartment. I'd instructed them to make contact while I handled the situation with Justin and Jillian's return, but instead of Jeremy walking into their initial trap, it had been Meredith who'd found them in her apartment instead. After that mishap, they made the wise decision to only encounter Jeremy at his work, so as to avoid another confrontation with the demon bitch herself.

Finally, tonight, they had tracked the two back to their apartment and after watching Meredith slink away, they had been able to get to him without any interference. He was now standing in my room with wide eyes, a gagged mouth, and his hands tied behind his back. I hated securing him like this, but since we couldn't bite him and use our sedative to keep him calm, we were left with no other choice.

"Jeremy. Please don't be afraid. We're not going to hurt you. We're only here to help reunite you with your daughter, and in the process, save our family."

I nodded to Bryce to remove the gag.

Jeremy stood calmly as he looked between us. "What the fuck are you talking about? I don't have a daughter yet. My fiancé is only a few weeks pregnant."

I immediately realized that trying to explain our situation wasn't going to help. I only hoped that during his transition process, his memories would fully return. So, without further delay, I launched myself at him and buried my fangs into his neck. The sedative of eternal life flowed into his veins as his body went slack in my arms. As soon as he took his last breath, I placed him on the couch and entered the bedroom we had prepared.

I immediately lay down on the operating table and let Nicholas hook up the transfusion equipment. From Evangeline's explanation I knew Jeremy's demon blood would cause me to drift dark. Therefore, my plan was to remove it from my system as fast as I could by performing a quick blood wash. Hopefully it would work and I could avoid losing myself and ultimately end up facing the true death at her hands.

Just before my mind started to blur, I instructed the boys, "If this doesn't work, take Jeremy to The Rising Pit and tell Evangeline everything. Let her know where I am and that I accept what she has to do." Their clipped nods indicated they understood.

I closed my eyes and tried to blank my thoughts while the medical equipment did its job. I didn't want any undue stress to impede the process because the faster we knew if this was going to work, the faster we could move forward with helping Jeremy adjust to his new life as our hybrid.

I felt groggy...hazy, but tried to remain still as the second round of machines kicked in. I could feel the blood moving in and out of my veins in a rhythmic push and pull. Suddenly I was lulled to sleep like a baby listening to a lullaby.

Upon waking, the first thing I thought of was how Evangeline was going to be upset by my decision. I hoped I could make her understand that she wasn't the only Sire who had a clan to protect. I looked around and found Bryce and Nicolas staring at me from the other side of the room. I assumed the fact that I remembered their names and what we were doing here was a good indication that the process had worked.

Bryce walked over and flipped off the equipment's switch as Nicholas asked, "How are you feeling?"

I sat up to gain my bearings. "I feel great actually. How long have I been out?"

"You dozed off briefly and drifted dark and back again a few times throughout the process, but overall, it's only been about an hour."

"Wow. That's great. That gives us plenty of time to get to The Rising Pit. I need to speak with Evangeline right away. Let's get Jeremy loaded into the truck and out of here while he completes his transition. I don't want him waking up in a building full of people, or with his demon fiancé directly overhead and hell-bent on finding him."

All three of us rushed around in a frenzy, packing up the medical equipment and wiping the place clean. Unlike Evangeline, I didn't plan to keep this apartment for further use.

We loaded the truck, securing Jeremy in the back seat, and headed directly to The Rising Pit.

* * * * *

(Jeremy)

After returning home from the movie I was ready to join my beautiful fiancé in bed when suddenly I was overwhelmed with exhaustion. The minute my head hit the pillow I was out like a light. Which was now one of the many reasons I was completely confused by my current predicament.

I was bound and gagged and standing in a different apartment with Bryce and Nicholas, my new clients, looking at another man I had not yet met. He was speaking to me about my daughter and how I could "save his family." *Good lord, I must be dreaming.*

Bryce removed the gag from my mouth and I told them I didn't have a daughter. They all looked at me with a sense of confusion.

Suddenly, the strange man launched himself across the room and bit the side of my neck. I didn't even have a chance to move before he was on me. I felt the warm trickle of some sort of serum filter into my veins. It immediately caused me to relax and forget any thoughts of fighting back. My mind became a haze of images as I felt myself bleed out.

I assumed I'd wake up back in my bed with Meredith tucked in beside me, but what I found when my eyes opened was a man shoving his arm into my mouth as the vehicle I was in jostled down the highway. I had no control over what I was doing and no idea where I was, but as the warm liquid flowed down my throat and the salty taste of his blood hit my tongue everything snapped into place.

I wasn't dreaming. William was my Sire, and I was now a vampire. *No...that's not right.* A hybrid. I was a demon and so was my daughter, Rose. My wife, Loraine, had been human and we'd been perfectly happy until *Meredith* ruined all our lives.

I raised my head from William's arm and screamed into the air. I could see everything clearly now, as if my transformation wiped out all the lies that previously layered my brain. I remembered the conversation with my daughter in which she'd explained everything to me. Meredith had killed the love of my life, then later set up Rose, causing her to go on the run. We were all demons and Meredith had obviously succeeded in controlling me, since she'd successfully erased my own daughter from my mind.

Another howl burst from my mouth as a darkness settled within my chest. I would hunt and kill this woman, this bitch, who'd ruined my *entire* life. A bitch whose blood I could currently smell riding the air currents around me.

I snapped my head up and took in my surroundings. I was in an SUV that sat parked on the edge of The Rising Pit's parking lot. It only took a moment for me to pinpoint Meredith. She was standing right in front of the club, surrounded by vampires and demons.

With a animalistic roar I burst through the roof of the truck and found that not only had the transformation changed my thoughts, it had changed my body as well. I had massive white wings that carried me into the air and sharp fangs that came to smooth points just below my lips.

I hovered over the scene for a split second before the demons started to run. I knew they were part of Meredith's army just from the smell they all carried. I swooped down and ripped the first two apart before landing only yards away from the woman who'd destroyed my life.

CHAPTER THIRTY-SEVEN

Right as Rain

(Christian)

I glanced at the clock to see if Rose and I had enough time to make love again before the sun rose. *Yes!* It was only 5:30 a.m. and the sun wouldn't be lighting the sky for another two hours.

I stared at Rose's naked body as she returned from the bathroom. Her wings shifted softly as she walked, and her pure white hair held a silver shimmer that reminded me of Loraine. She was so beautiful and I knew I'd never be happier than I was in this moment.

"I love you, Rose, and I'm going to tell you every single day."

"Wow. *Every* day for...forever? That's a lot!" She giggled, as her eyes brightened.

Talk about a new twist in our drifting. It now seemed that whenever our emotions flared, we both took on the golden hue from our consort bond. I was wondering what the others would think about it when a massive roar sounded above us.

Rose's head snapped up as she sniffed the air, looking very much like the hybrid she was. "Demons!" she exclaimed. Her wings flared and eyes went wide and in the next second we both flew into our clothes and raced out of the room.

As we stepped through the front door, we were met with a raging battle.

My clan was standing near the front of the club, watching as a winged creature dove through the crowd, ripping multiple demons to shreds. Meredith was in the middle of the chaos, trying to hide behind anyone close enough to offer her the slightest level of protection. It didn't take long before the ground was littered with body parts and she was the only demon left standing. We all watched as she made her plea.

"Please, Jeremy. Don't kill me...remember, I'm going to have your baby."

Holy shit!! This was Rose's father. I stood in shocked silence and wondered how Jeremy had become a hybrid. I was about to pose this very question when I looked at Rose and knew it didn't matter.

She was smiling from ear to ear with tears in her eyes.

* * * * *

(Rose)

Seeing my dad as a good hybrid, like me, made my chest burst with pride. I'd missed him so much, and after almost walking away and losing myself, and him, to this disgusting woman in front of me, I could hardly contain myself.

"Dad!"

I ran to meet him in the open space between my clan and the carnage before us.

"Oh, Rose. Are you okay?"

I buried my head in his chest and felt myself grow a little warmer as tears of joy filled my eyes. "Yes. I'm fine *now*."

I hugged him tightly before pulling back to get a good look at him. "How are you? And how in the world did you become a hybrid?"

Before he answered, he flew to Meredith, who'd taken a few steps in the direction of the surrounding forest, and lifted her into the air by the throat. I laughed out loud as she dangled from his grip like a wet noodle. She kicked and yelled, but Dad silenced her with a quick shake as he bared his fangs and growled in her face.

Turning his attention back to me, he called out, "William! Could you come out here please. It looks like you have some explaining to do."

We all watched as William and two of his vampires climbed out of the truck that was parked at the lot's farthest edge. A truck with a huge hole in its roof.

"William, will you be so kind as to explain to everyone how we arrived *here*?" Dad asked as he motioned to himself with his free hand.

William proceeded to explain that after Evie told him about the demons and what her plan was, he'd decided to follow in her footsteps, using Jeremy to protect his own clan.

He'd specifically paid special attention to how she worried that Christian had turned dark due to Rose's blood and formulated a way to avoid that part of the process. By performing a blood transfusion and immediately cleaning the demon blood from his system, there would be no contaminates to cause him or Jeremy to drift dark once he awoke and fed from him. His plan had worked perfectly, but it was when Jeremy's anger and emotions flared over the realization of all Meredith had done, that his wings literally sprouted forth the moment he burst through the roof of their truck.

"Wow." I didn't know what else to say. Christian and Evie had made their way forward to join me during William's rapid explanation. As Christian placed his hand around my waist, I felt him nudge my mind with a question; one I repeated to Dad immediately.

"So what are we going to do with her?" I pointed to Meredith, who was still dangling like a rag doll in my father's grip.

"I'll leave that up to you, Rose. She killed your mother and has been after you and your clan for months. Not to mention tricking and controlling me. It's your choice."

Everyone stared at me while I contemplated. A day ago I would have ripped out her throat and drawn pictures in her blood and not even blinked, but now...I wasn't sure how I felt or what the right thing to do was. But, before I could truly process my feelings, something strange started to happen.

Meredith started convulsing, causing my dad to lose his grip. She hit the ground hard, but instead of fleeing, she remained coiled as her entire body twisted and popped. The sounds of her bones snapping and cracking, accompanied by her horrible screams, filled the air and blood started pouring out of her mouth, nose, and ears.

Everyone took a step back in an effort to distance themselves from the gruesome scene. The startled expressions we all wore confirmed that no one had any idea of what the hell was going on.

I quickly put my scanning ability to use to see if I could understand what was causing such a horrible reaction. Christian, Evie, and Dax must have been doing the same thing because as I looked up we all shared a sense of shocked understanding.

"What's happening, Rose?" Dad asked.

"It's the baby. Your transformation into the hybrid has affected him through your bond. He's changing and it's caused Meredith's body to reject him and the blood she's ingested. I'm sorry, Dad, they're not going to make it."

The stoic expression that settled on my father's face mocked the feelings of the entire clan. I was about to say something like, *"Maybe it's for the best,"* when suddenly, I caught a whiff of more demons. I snapped my head towards the forest and watched as two elderly women emerged from its edge.

With their hands raised, one announced, "We come in peace."

As they approached the macabre scene, horror showed in both of their eyes. They stood over Meredith, crying as they watched her contorted form struggle for its last breath.

"I'm Meredith's grandmother, and this is Lupé, an elder and demon in Meredith's *army*." Tears slid down her cheeks as she gazed at her now dead granddaughter. "Lupé came to me tonight and explained Meredith's plans." She shook her head. "I tried to warn her that drinking human blood would be the downfall of our race, but I had no idea it would end like this. Her greed for power and immortality caused her to experience a severe case of bloodlust, one she could no longer control."

She wiped her face and reached for Lupé's hand before continuing.

"Drinking blood is something demons are no longer meant to do...that is your lot in life, not ours. Meredith chose not to heed my warnings and paid the ultimate price, but it's our hope that with this *ending* we can start anew. Lupé and I will *never* allow our kind to drink again and will share what's happened here with the elders of our race. We have no quarrel with you or those like you. Will you accept our offer of peace and agree to a truce between us?"

Evie started to walk towards the women but paused when she reached Christian's side. Placing her hand on his back, she smiled and gave him an encouraging nod.

Christian walked towards the women and extended his hand. "We accept."

And just like that, the threat that had plagued my family for the last year had come to an end. Christian hugged me, then released me into my dad's embrace. The rest of the clan, including William and his vampires, starting piling the body parts on top of Meredith's remains as the demon elders simply walked away. We all stood back when Terrance flicked his lighter and tossed it onto them. It was fitting, after everything Meredith had put him through, too.

We all watched as the flames licked the sky. I knew there were other demons out there, but with the ability my father and I possessed to *literally* sniff them out, none of them could threaten us ever again, even if they did choose to break the truce. I looked at Christian and gave him a slight smile, as our "battle" came to a fiery end. My entire family was finally safe, and while our wings limited my father and me to only coming out at night—just like true vampires—we were free to live our lives together and without fear, and *that* fact alone made everything right as rain.

The End

Author's Note

As I stare at the words, *"The End,"* I feel a hint of sadness but also one of renewed wonder at the thought of my next adventure. While it's hard to say goodbye to Rose and Christian, I feel that they will always be a part of me in whatever story I'm trying to write. I will carry with me the strength these characters have in whatever else I do, for they are such an inspiration to me. The devotion they have for one another is so subtle throughout the series, that sometimes you forget that they are basically newlyweds. They seem instead like that old married couple who has been through so much together, that they could complete each other's sentences, or come to an understanding with just a simple look. That is Christian and Rose; truly, madly, deeply in love with one another, and I with them. Goodbye my friends. ♥

Turn the page for an excerpt from

Raven's Breath

by

Tish Thawer

1

Sirens blared, cutting through the still night, while I watched from the shadows. A man who'd just been hit by a taxi lay bleeding on the frigid, grime covered ground. People began to gather and were staring at the gruesome scene, while the driver of the taxi sat on the curb, crying into his hands.

I scanned the crowd, singling out who'd seen death before and who hadn't.

I could always tell.

My attention snapped back to the dying man when he took his last breath. Images began to take shape in his mind; images that due to my *job*, I, too, could see.

Snapshots of him riding a motorcycle for the first time, of him falling in love, of his big successful promotion at work...all images of him. It was the usual replay of one's life flashing before his eyes.

When the replay stopped, it was time for me to go to work.

I stepped out of the shadows and took two steps in his direction. To the people watching, his wide eyes marked his final passing, but to me they continued to grow as he took in my features: dark hair blowing in the wind, a curvaceous body wrapped in tight black leather, and large wings the color of the night sky. No one could see me but him, for he now resided in the netherworld...in my world.

I extended my hand and offered my usual greeting. "My name is Raven, and I'm here to help you find peace." He reached for me, then glanced back to take a final look at his body.

"Am I really dead?"

"Yes."

"And you are..."

"The Grim Reaper."

This was the exact conversation I'd had with thousands of souls, which was why I knew that *now* would be the best time to comfort him, before he got scared to death—no pun intended——and tried to flee from me.

I extended my wings and let my divine light radiate from within. "There's nothing to fear."

This usually worked since I looked more like an angel with wings than the old man with a scythe that most people envisioned. Maybe that's why I'd been chosen to become the first female Reaper in history; the boys had been losing too many souls.